Adam's eyes dark **very obvious inne. .. uggle.** "You sure?"

His voice was quiet and deep, a little rough. Not demanding or aggressive, which would have instantly had her shields snapping into place. Despite the almost physical yearning rising up in her to say, "No, I'm not sure. Take me anyway," Sam found herself nodding and shaking her head at the same time.

Yikes. Way to be decisive.

Confused and tempted—so darn tempted, especially when disappointment flashed across his starkly handsome face—she bit her lip and nodded reluctantly.

Sending her one last searching look, he turned away and stepped forward as the doors opened. He was almost through the doorway when something inside her snapped. She gave a strangled gurgle that sounded like "Wait!" and before she could reconsider, she was spinning Adam around and pushing him against the steel frame.

Sliding up against all that warm hardness, she rose onto her toes and, for the second time that night, caught his mouth in a kiss because she suddenly couldn't face the thought of him walking away.

Dear Reader,

So often we feel like our lives are barreling out of control with a dramatic wipeout in sight and no way to stop the coming disaster. Samantha Jefferies is way overdue for a major life change, but it takes walking in on her fiancé—in flagrante delicto with his assistant, Ronald—to kick the whole catastrophe off.

In the space of one weekend, she loses her fiancé, is forced into a bridesmaid dress more suited for prom and dances barefoot in an upmarket hotel bar after lining up a selection of shooters from the bar menu because it's something she's never done before.

It would have been fine if she'd left off stretching herself there. But oh, no, she has to compound her sins by pretending she's free-spirited "Amanda," who's accustomed to kissing hot strangers she's met in a bar and spending a wild night of passion together—all after helping him deliver a baby in a stuck elevator. Besides, what else is a woman named Amanda decked out in a hot-pink thong under a hot-pink bridesmaid dress supposed to do?

Happy reading!

Lucy

TEMPTED BY
THE HEART SURGEON

———

LUCY RYDER

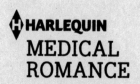

HARLEQUIN

MEDICAL
ROMANCE

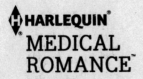

HARLEQUIN®
MEDICAL ROMANCE™

Recycling programs
for this product may
not exist in your area.

ISBN-13: 978-1-335-14972-5

Tempted by the Heart Surgeon

Copyright © 2020 by Bev Riley

This edition published by arrangement with Harlequin Books S.A.

For questions and comments about the quality of this book, please contact us at CustomerService@Harlequin.com.

Harlequin Enterprises ULC
22 Adelaide St. West, 40th Floor
Toronto, Ontario M5H 4E3, Canada
www.Harlequin.com

Printed in U.S.A.

With two beautiful daughters, **Lucy Ryder** has had to curb her adventurous spirit and settle down. But because she's easily bored by routine, she's turned to writing as a creative outlet, and to romances because "What else is there other than chocolate?" Characterized by friends and family as a romantic cynic, Lucy can't write serious stuff to save her life. She loves creating characters who are funny, romantic and just a little cynical.

Books by Lucy Ryder

Harlequin Medical Romance

Rebels of Port St. John's

Rebel Doc on Her Doorstep
Resisting Her Commander Hero

Resisting Her Rebel Hero
Tamed by Her Army Doc's Touch
Falling at the Surgeon's Feet
Caught in a Storm of Passion
Pregnant by the Playboy Surgeon

Visit the Author Profile page at Harlequin.com.

To my editor, Sareeta Domingo, who's had an
incredibly rough year, and to Sheila Hodgson,
who stepped in and helped me through my own
rough year. Thank you, ladies. I wouldn't have
made it without your help.

CHAPTER ONE

SAMANTHA JEFFERIES GLANCED over her shoulder and ducked into the hotel bar, relieved to discover the place packed and the lights dim. Hopefully, she could hide from a very handsy and persistent groomsman, and take a break from the Wedding from Hell where she was one of eleven bridesmaids from an adolescent fantasy.

Eleven! Who the heck had eleven bridesmaids?

But then again, at least Stacey had her life together, while Sam's was falling apart. Taking a break from her Life from Hell sounded like an ideal plan. Maybe she could even pretend to be someone else for an hour or two. Pretend she hadn't seen what she'd seen, that she wasn't dressed like a prom escapee or that her own wedding wasn't a thing of the past. Or would be as soon as she informed her grandmother, she thought with a grimace.

And wasn't *that* going to be a thrill a minute. Considering her grandmother had—for once—

completely approved of Sam's fiancé, the old battle-ax would blow a gasket.

She didn't want to think about what her brother would say since he'd never *ever* had a life crisis.

Truthfully, it wasn't that her cousin's wedding was that bad, she admitted, heading for the bar counter farthest from the door—although if she had to endure one more girlish shriek and emotional outburst, she was likely to start screaming herself, and never stop.

It was just that she'd very recently—as in two days ago—walked into her fiancé's large and very tastefully decorated office, and caught him *in flagrante* with his PA.

His male PA.

And if that wasn't deserving of a long-overdue freak-out, it was the fact that she was now wearing an off-the-shoulder pink confection—*yeah, strawberry pink!*—its form-fitting bodice showcasing more curves than she was comfortable showing and drawing more masculine attention than she wanted.

The skirt, a short wide explosion of organza, left most of her long legs free and made her look a bit like a gawky flamingo on the lam from the San Diego Zoo.

Samantha Jefferies, granddaughter of Lilian Gilford, CEO of Gilford Pharmaceuticals and doyenne of Boston high society, would *never* be seen dead in something that would fit right into the chorus line of the Folies Bergère—*sans* feathered headdress, of course. Then again, that in itself might have endeared the outfit to her if not for the fact that she wanted to blend in, escape Mr. Hands, take a deep breath without popping the seams—or the strapless décolletage—and process the last three days with the hopes of salvaging her on-the-skids life.

In this dress, there wasn't a hope in hell of that happening.

Drawing on years of conditioning, Sam ignored the amused smirks and speculative glances and tossed her strappy sandals onto the bar counter. With an irritated tug on the stupid skirt, she slid onto an empty barstool.

As a newly advanced-age single, she might want to get with the program but she wanted to do it without flashing her very new, very scandalous pink thong. First thing on the agenda was to sample everything life had to offer before she was forced to trade her strappy highs for comfortable orthopedic lace-ups.

The bartender appeared before her, eyes smiling, brows arched as he took in her appearance. If not for the fact that he looked about twelve, she might have flirted a little to test her newly liberated wings.

"Lose your way to the prom, princess?"

"Not any more than you look old enough to serve alcohol," she drawled, smiling sweetly when she wanted to snarl, because if she had to field one more comment on her appearance, she might scream.

He sighed. Clearly it wasn't the first time someone had commented on his youthful appearance. "So what'll it be?"

"I'd like to see your shooters menu." Heck, if she was going to begin a new life as a swinging single, she might as well start with some "swingy" drink. She'd never set foot in a bar, let alone sampled a shooter. The granddaughter of Lilian Gilford and fiancée of Lawrence Winthrop the Third would never imbibe anything stronger than sherry.

Well that, she decided, wriggling on the barstool, was about to change, especially if it shocked the blue rinse right out of her grandmother's elegant hairdo.

Smirking—and clearly still smarting from the quip about his age—he demanded, "Your mom know you're in here ordering alcohol?"

"The menu, sonny," she drawled. "And make it snappy. You're losing tips here."

He laughed good-naturedly and slid the menu across the bar. "Sure thing, princess. So what'll it be?"

"I want you to start at the top and give me one of everything." Might as well go for broke.

Dr. Adam Knight saw her the moment she walked into the bar in a downtown upmarket San Francisco hotel. Frankly, he would have noticed her anywhere. In a place filled with hockey players and tables of rowdy Saturday-night revelers ready to rumble, she looked as out of place as a giant pink peony in a desert garden.

Nope, he thought, as she moved toward the long mahogany bar. She was all woman—from the top of her upswept, flower-sprinkled dark chestnut hair to smooth naked shoulders, a long elegant and straight-as-a-ruler back and down the mile-long legs to her bare feet. A pair of pink strappy four-inch sandals dangled from one slender finger.

"So," Adam heard his friend and colleague, Wes Kirkland, say behind him as he gestured with his beer to the vision in pink. "Ten bucks says she's from the mansion."

The other occupant of the table, a short slender brunette, took her eyes off her phone to demand, "Mansion? What mansion?" Her eyes narrowed on the object of their interest and after a short pause she snorted rudely. "You guys have a one-track mind. If you ask me, it looks like she's wandered in from a costume party."

Wes scoffed. "Dressed as what? A flamingo?"

Ignoring them, Adam watched as she leaned forward to exchange words with the bartender. Within minutes, he had a line of shot glasses in front of her. From this distance, Adam couldn't identify them but by the second shot, her Vegas showgirl legs were propped onto a nearby bar-stool. By the third, she was surrounded by hockey players all ordering shots and joining in what seemed to have become a shot party.

He saw the Peony laugh and shake her head, then grab the bar counter to keep from falling off her stool when one guy snaked an arm around her waist and tried to pull her toward him.

Another burly guy stepped in and for a mo-ment Adam thought there would be a violent tussle with her in the middle. She said some-thing that made the guys stop, patted them both on their big arms and slid off the stool to join a nearby group of women on the dance floor. The first guy followed and tried to tug her back, but she laughed and spun away, her long legs flash-ing as she attempted to lose herself among the dancers.

She wouldn't be lost for long, Adam thought with a grin. Not in that pink dress.

"Bet *I* could get her to dance," Wes announced confidently. "All I have to do is tell her I'm a doc-tor. Chicks love that."

"I think they love hockey players more," Janice snorted, gesturing to the women crowding around the players at the bar.

Listening to their banter with half an ear, Adam watched as a big hockey player cornered her and wrapped an arm around her waist. She shook her head at something he said and rolled her eyes good-naturedly when he tugged her into a dance, finessing her around the floor like he was weaving a puck through a line of defensemen toward the posts. He must have reached his imaginary goal because he suddenly spun her around and dramatically bent her low over his arm like a cheesy Lothario in a classic movie.

She laughed, the sound low and husky as she tried to shove his face away from her cleavage. Then her gaze locked with Adam's and he felt it like a one-two punch to his solar plexus. The moment caught and held, stretching between them with invisible bands. Bands that abruptly snapped when the guy whipped her upright and around, his hands sliding aggressively over her curves.

Before Adam could object on her behalf, or recover from that odd moment of connection, she shoved the hockey player away and stumbled backward, tripping over the couple who'd moved in behind her. With a startled squeak, she toppled.

Right into Adam's lap.

Instinctively wrapping an arm around her to keep her from landing on the floor, he murmured, "Gotcha."

One minute Sam was wrestling with the clumsy hockey stud, the next she'd tumbled right into someone sitting at a dance-floor table. She gave a startled yelp as one hard arm snaked around her midriff and hauled her back against an even harder, warmer chest, cutting off her air.

In some dark, purely feminine corner of her mind, she enjoyed the sensation of having a man's arms around her again—of a hard masculine chest and muscular thighs cradling her—while she twisted to right herself and find her feet.

Her elbow connected with something hard and the guy behind her exhaled in a softly groaned *oomph.* She froze, the automatic apology dying on her lips. Oh, God, could this evening get any worse? First, the groomsman from hell, then the clumsy hockey stud with one thing on his mind. And now this.

Beneath her organza tulle bottom, hard thighs flexed, leaving her weak, shaky and shocked that she was reacting physically to a stranger she couldn't even see. Twisting around, she came

face-to-face with the guy she'd locked eyes with
for that one startling instant.

And boy, he was even better looking up close
and the right way up. High forehead, straight as
an arrow nose, slashing cheekbones and a strong
jaw beneath warm coppery gold skin gave his
face a strength and nobility that more than hinted
at his Native American ancestry.

Something within her stilled. And then, as
though drawn by a will not her own, her gaze
dropped to his mouth where a smile tugged at the
sculpted lips a couple of inches from her own.
Probably with amusement at suddenly finding
a woman in pink giving him a spontaneous and
inept lap dance, she decided dazedly.

"S'cuse me," she gasped. Unable to stop staring at his mouth, she hoped he'd interpret her
breathlessness as a result of being spun and
tossed around, and not because, even in a room
seething with testosterone, his pheromones
pinged off her radar like a nuclear blast.

The next thing she noticed was his hair, thick
and straight and jet-black as it fell almost to his
shoulders. Her fingers twitched with an almost
agonizing urge to slide through all that black
silk. She curled them instead into the hard muscles and bones of his shoulders, and she wasn't
the least bit disappointed.

Hmmm, she thought, flexing her fingers experimentally. *Big and solid and—*

Almost as though he could read her thoughts, his smile grew and strong white teeth flashed in the semi-darkness. "No harm done," he drawled with a chuckle, his deep baritone sending a delicious shiver sliding up the length of her spine. A large warm hand tightened on her hip and her belly bottomed out, leaving her relieved she was sitting because even her knees wobbled in response to that heated look.

Oh, boy. He was easily the hottest guy she'd ever met, effortlessly oozing sex appeal from every pore that might have had her as tongue-tied as a thirteen-year-old if not for the very lovely buzz she had going.

Whatever it was, the shooters or the champagne she'd tossed back earlier, she found herself incomprehensibly glad for her clumsiness. If she was kick-starting her new life as a single, she couldn't have asked for a better way to test her nonexistent flirting skills.

She slid her gaze over his strong jawline and skimmed up the length of his straight nose to heavily lashed eyes the color of her grandfather's favorite whiskey. And just as it had rushed straight to her head the first time she'd tasted the expensive drink, she lost her breath now as the world tilted.

"S-sorry," she murmured, falling into their potent depths. "I—"

"Hey!" someone complained behind her, jolting her out of the sensual trance she'd been slipping into without a whimper. "Get your mitts off my girl." It was the lumbering hockey stud, closing a hand roughly over her shoulder as he tried to yank her off her perch.

With a shrug of her shoulder, Sam dislodged his hand and wrapped her arms around the gorgeous hot guy's neck. Leaning forward, she begged, "Save me," against his lips and did something she'd never done before. She slid her fingers into thick cool hair and kissed a stranger.

She might have been shocked by her uncharacteristic behavior if not for the two—or was that three?—shooters and two glasses of champagne and the past forty-eight hours. Forty-eight hours since she'd discovered the reason her fiancé had insisted on waiting for the wedding night before he saw her naked. Forty-eight hours of wondering why she hadn't seen what everyone else knew. That her handsome, buff, blond fiancé *was* interested in sex—just not with her, because he was having an affair with his assistant. A guy named Ronnie.

If not for that image stuck in her head, Sam was sure she wouldn't be snuggled in some hot guy's lap, contemplating throwing a lifetime of caution to the wind. Or then again, it could easily be the amused expression in his amber eyes that dared her to plunge right in. She was single after all, and hadn't she just decided to take life by the horns instead of meekly allowing her grandmother to direct her path?

Whatever it was, it was suddenly so hugely liberating that she experienced a moment's dizziness. Besides, she was heading back to Boston in the morning and would never see any of these people ever again.

But staring into his bourbon-colored eyes, the "something" that had stilled within her sparked abruptly to life and for just an instant it was as though—as though she knew him. Before she could tell herself how ridiculous that sounded, her heart leaped and thundered as elation rose within her along with a need that was as frightening as it was wildly thrilling.

The guy stilled. His big hands closed over her shoulders and for one mortifying moment, Sam thought he'd push her away. Then he cupped the back of her head with one hand, the other dropping to nudge her hips closer to his.

And the next instant, he was kissing her back.

The instant that generously sculpted mouth opened beneath hers and applied a slight suction, it took only a half a dozen frantic heartbeats for her to lose her mind.

And for him to completely own her.

Or the kiss, she corrected dazedly. *Own the kiss.* Because owning her a minute after they'd met was about as farfetched as looking into a stranger's eyes and imagining that soul-click.

In some dim corner of her mind, she heard someone say, "Forget her big boy, I'm a much better dancer," then the heat of his body seeped into hers and the rest of the bar faded away, leaving her in a world she'd only ever dreamed about. It was as though she'd finally discovered fire after wandering through a frozen wasteland for nearly twenty-eight years. Finally experiencing for herself what everyone else knew.

His lips were softer than she'd expected, warmer. A sigh escaped her when his tongue slid along the length of hers, setting off a chain reaction that had her squirming with instant heat. Shifting closer, she reveled in the taste of him— slightly bitter from the beer he'd been drinking and something else. Something dark and delicious and uniquely male.

Uniquely *him*.

Then the kiss turned hot and carnal, and it was all she could do to keep up because her blood caught fire. The heat of the hard thighs against her bottom burned through her awful pink dress to her fluttering core and set all her senses aflame.

In all her secret fantasies, she'd never been kissed like this—with lips and tongue and scraping teeth. Like he wanted to consume her right there in public, in front of all these strangers.

And she was tempted to let him.

It was that last thought that had her jerking away to stare at him in shock. "I…uh… I'm s-sorry," she stammered, rudely returned to reality like she'd been doused with icy water. What the heck was she doing kissing a guy like they were alone and had known each other longer than a couple of minutes?

He stared back at her through heavy-lidded eyes almost black with arousal and murmured, "I'm not," in a voice so rough and tight with lust that she shivered. One of those delicious shivers that started at the base of her spine and rolled over her body in deep luscious waves, leaving her senses heightened and her body humming.

Heat swept up from her jittery belly, filling her chest with the champagne she'd consumed before racing up her throat into her face in a hot wave she wasn't altogether certain was embarrassment. Or maybe not *just* embarrassment.

Then out the corner of her eye, she caught movement and turned to see Mr. Hands, the groomsman, bearing down on her like the IRS intent on an audit.

Dammit, she cursed silently. Trust him to find

her here of all places, just when she was finally beginning to enjoy the anonymity of the dimly lit bar.

The condemnation in Jared's eyes had her own eyes narrowing in an uncharacteristic display of temper. Decked out in his vintage wedding tuxedo, he looked ridiculously pretentious in comparison to soft faded jeans and a plain white T-shirt stretched across broad shoulders that needed no padding to look wide and solid and safe.

"Amanda," he clipped out, probably annoyed that she was fondling another man when she'd been evading *his* hot sweaty hands all weekend. "What are you doing here? I've been looking everywhere for you." *Hoping to maneuver her into a tight corner, no doubt.*

It was on the tip of her tongue to tell him for the thousandth time that her name was Samantha not Amanda when she was gripped by an almost savage need to shock that supercilious look right off his face. She suddenly wanted to rebel against everything in her life that kept her from being the woman she wanted to be. She wanted to be bold and face life head-on instead of timidly letting it control her.

It was tempting to dispel once and for all the prim-and-proper image that had been drummed into her since childhood and behave like a *nor-*

mal person for once. A woman with needs and emotions; someone light-years away from the mousey, emotionless and perpetually elegant and dignified woman her grandmother expected her to be.

Well, she thought, wiggling suggestively in the hot guy's lap and giving herself a hot flash in the process. *Damn elegant and to hell with dignified.* She'd left that behind in Boston the moment she'd turned away from the sight of her fiancé and his boy toy to walk calmly from the room, shutting the door quietly behind her, leaving them in no doubt that the wedding was off.

Ignoring Jared, she cupped the hot guy's handsome angular jaw between her palms and smiled into his intoxicating eyes before closing the gap between their lips to place a soft lingering kiss on his mouth. Her blood heated anew when he responded with flattering enthusiasm and smoothed his big hands up the length of her spine.

Shivering deliciously, she gave in to the wild, wanton creature inside of her. After drowning in the taste of him, she reluctantly broke the kiss, her tingling lips remaining on his for a moment longer before she eased back an inch. Staring into his eyes, she memorized the hot potent expression there and the way it made her feel. Like a hot-blooded woman a red-blooded man might desire. Just like a woman bent on experiencing everything life had to offer.

"Duty calls," she murmured, lightly tracing his bottom lip with one finger. Then with real regret, she slid off his lap, grateful for his supporting hands when her knees wobbled and her head spun.

Whoa. No more shooters for you.

Or maybe that should be no more intoxicating kisses from hot strangers. But damn. She really wanted more of that.

"Sure you won't stay?" he asked quietly, his eyes locked on hers. She was tempted—*boy was she tempted.* Then Jared called, "Amanda," in that peremptory tone she suddenly decided she hated, because it was exactly the tone her grandmother used when she felt Sam wasn't living up to Gilford standards. Just as Jared was exactly the kind of man the old battle-ax would approve of: good family, great pedigree, oodles of old money.

And boring as hell.

She shook her head regretfully. "I…can't."

His gaze, dark and seductive, held hers and myriad messages passed between them that she struggled to interpret. "My loss," he murmured, his big hand warm and comforting on hers until her fingers slid free.

CHAPTER TWO

ADAM POCKETED HIS key card and headed for the bank of elevators at the far end of the lobby. After the Peony—Amanda, the stiff had called her—left, the evening seemed to fizzle.

He wouldn't go so far as to say he'd felt bereft watching her walk away but it had been pretty damn close. As if something meaningful was slipping from his grasp. And he was letting it.

His grandmother would have said their souls had clicked but Adam knew just how corny that sounded. Much cornier than if he'd just admitted that his hormones had suddenly awakened from a long hibernation and said, *Mine*.

But that was just his neglected libido talking, he admitted wryly. Besides, he was getting too old for one-night stands, even if tall long-legged women dressed like prom queens suddenly seemed to have become a very personal and surprising fantasy.

He arrived just as the doors were closing and

he thrust his hand into the opening, causing the doors to bounce, then jerk back open. He stepped forward, an apology dying on his lips when he caught sight of an explosion of pink and wide startled eyes. Eyes so startlingly blue they seemed to glow beneath their luxurious fringe of dark lashes.

Soft lips parted in a soundless gasp and she stared back at him.

His gaze swept from the top of her tousled chestnut hair to her elegant feet, which were no longer bare. The pink strappy sandals she'd been carrying earlier made her long legs appear even longer. She looked good even in the harsh elevator lights, especially when his frank appraisal caused color to rush beneath soft creamy skin.

That embarrassed self-consciousness was in direct contrast to the bold seductress of a couple hours ago. It caught and held his interest even more than the pink peony dress and long limbs.

Abruptly realizing that he was preventing the doors from closing, and that the elevator's other very pregnant occupant was staring at him with wide-eyed interest, Adam murmured, "Evening ladies," and stepped into the car to punch his floor number. Once the doors slid closed, he propped a shoulder against the wall and studied the woman he'd met in the bar, looking at him as though she hadn't had her tongue in his mouth a couple of hours ago.

"Um...hi again," she said, trying not to squirm even as heat rose up her neck into her face. Her voice, as low and husky as he remembered, gave him a few bad moments when he recalled the way she'd murmured *save me* against his mouth before kissing his socks off.

"I see you escaped your jailer."

She looked momentarily confused. "My jail—? Oh, you mean Jared? Nope." She grimaced. "We're not together," she explained as the very pregnant young woman—also in an explosion of eye-popping pink tulle and organza—snorted.

"No woman in her right mind would *be* with Jared," the young mother-to-be said, as she sucked in a shaky breath and rubbed her enormous belly. "He's an accountant and you know how *they* are."

"Daphne," Amanda whispered aghast, grimacing an apology as Adam's smile widened.

"What?"

Amanda flicked her gaze in his direction as the elevator rose. "Maybe *he's* an accountant," he heard her whisper.

Before he could reassure them that he wasn't, Daphne shook her head firmly. "Nope," she whispered back loudly. "No way. Just look at him. Does any of *that* say accountant to you?"

"How do you know?" Amanda demanded sotto voce, coloring beneath his stare. "It's not like accountants *look* a certain way."

"Of course they do," Daphne argued. "There's Pete and Rowland and don't forget Jared and his brother Mark and oh—"

The last was in response to the jolt as the elevator came to an abrupt and unexpected stop. It swayed violently, prompting the two women to clutch frantically at the rail behind them to keep from being thrown to the floor.

The lights flickered once, brightened and just before they blinked out completely, he saw Daphne's eyes widen as she grabbed her belly. "Uh-oh," she said, and Adam, who'd spent enough time during his internship catching babies, knew instantly what it meant.

"Don't panic Daph," he heard Amanda say tightly. "I'm sure it's only a computer glitch. We'll be on our way in a minute and then you can relax in a nice warm bath while I call Stan—"

"That's not what the uh-oh was for," Daphne interrupted on a thin wail. "I think my water just broke."

"It's all right," Amanda soothed. "No one can blame you for not having control of your bladder

at a time like this. I'm sure…um…" She paused
and Adam could feel her looking his way.

"Adam," he supplied helpfully.

"Oh. Right," she said in a tone that told Adam
she was recalling in perfect detail that she'd been
up close and personal with a man whose name
she didn't know. "I'm sure…um… Adam will
forgive you this one lapse. Besides, it's entirely
understandable in a woman who's almost ten
months pregnant."

"Eight months," Daphne said with a tight, dry
laugh.

Adam drawled, "I think she means she's in
labor," turning to feel for the emergency button
on the panel.

The emergency lights finally flickered on just
in time for him to see Amanda staring at him in
open-mouthed horror.

"Labor?" she squeaked, her eyes wide as she
dropped her gaze to stare at the other woman's
swollen belly. Her expression told him she half
expected an alien to pop out any second. "But—
but you can't," she said fiercely, clutching Daphne's arm. "It's not time. Tell him," she ordered
frantically. "Tell the hunk he's mistaken. Tell that
baby it's not time, because if I remember correctly, babies are supposed to stay there nine
months. *Nine months, Daph*." She broke off and
sucked in a shaky breath. "Besides," she con-

tinued tightly after a short battle with her slipping control. "Stan isn't even here. You can't give
birth without Stan."

"Yeah, well—" Daphne wheezed out a laugh
as she clutched her belly "—I don't think this kid
is about to wait for Stan to get here. *Oh, God*,"
she wailed and grabbed Amanda's arm. "I hope
you know something about birthing babies, hon,
'cause you're it."

Amanda yelped as her arm turned white
around the younger woman's grip. Adam eyed
her curiously, because it was obvious that she
was battling to remain in control of a situation
that had all the hallmarks of going to hell in a
handbasket. "I know zip about babies, Daphne,
let alone how to help one into this world."

"Fortunately," Adam said briskly, digging out
his cell phone to toss at Amanda. "I do." He
checked his watch while she fumbled the catch,
finally looking up to find them both staring at
him as though he'd suggested something inde-
cent. "I'm a doctor," he told them absently, as he
calculated that it had been about four minutes
since the last contraction.

Amanda looked relieved. "A doctor? Please
tell me you're a gynecologist."

"Call 911," he ordered, ignoring her question
and taking Daphne's arm. He didn't think either
of them needed to know he was a cardiothoracic

surgeon. He gently pushed Daphne to her hands and knees. "This position will help," he murmured, briskly rubbing her back. "Explain the situation," he addressed the woman huddled in the corner with a deer-in-the-headlights look on her face. "Tell them to send an ambulance and the fire brigade."

"Fire brigade?" the two women yelped, staring at him with similar expressions of horror.

"You mean there might be a fire?" Daphne squealed, slapping at Adam's hands as she shot upright to glare at him. "I am *not* giving birth in the middle of a fire!"

"No," Amanda said, her wide blue eyes clinging to his as she punched in the emergency numbers with shaking fingers. "I think it's in case maintenance can't get the computers rebooted in time and they have to break us out of here."

Adam nodded reassuringly. "That's right," he soothed gently, reassessing his Peony as Daphne blew out a long breath and grunted, "Breaking us out sounds good. Can they do it now?"

"Soon," Adam promised. "For now, all you need to do is concentrate on breathing through the contractions. No pushing, okay? Just breathing."

After relaying the information to the 911 dispatcher, Amanda turned narrowed eyes on him. "You better know what you're d-doing," she stuttered in a fierce undertone over Daphne's heaving form. "Because I wasn't kidding. I h-have no idea what I'm supposed to do other than b-boil water and get fresh towels before hiding until it's all over."

Adam grabbed her hand and tugged her down to the floor, guiding her hand to Daphne's lower back. "Trust me," he said cheerfully, a quick grin lighting his face. "I know what I'm doing." Maybe she'd stay calm if he gave her something to do. "Look at me," he ordered softly when he caught the quick panicked sound of her breathing. Her wide eyes flew to his and he said firmly, "Concentrate on breathing evenly. Can you do that?"

She swallowed, a quick spasmodic movement of her throat, before nodding. "Good," he murmured with an encouraging grin. "Now rub. It probably feels like her back is breaking. Keep rubbing and don't worry. Daphne and her baby know what to do."

"I do?" Daphne panted, sounding a little shaky. "I hate to break it to you, handsome, but this is my first time. I have no idea what to expect."

Amanda gulped, and Adam caught sight of her pink tongue emerging to swipe nervously across her soft plump lip. "I thought you said you went to Lamaze classes?"

"I did," Daphne grunted. "But they didn't say

anything about giving birth in an elevator. Nothing," she yelped, squeezing her eyes closed, "in any of the books I read said anything…about… *giving birth in an elevator*." Her voice got louder until she was almost yelling.

Amanda flinched, her eyes wide as she frantically rubbed the other woman's back and flicked a look at him. "Shouldn't she be lying down?" she hissed, but Adam shook his head, enjoying the drama despite himself.

"This position is more natural for now. Ideally, when the time comes, she should be squatting."

Both women looked appalled. "Squatting?" Daphne screeched, "If you think I'm squatting, buster, you're insane. In fact," she batted their hands away and grabbed the railing behind her before hauling herself to her feet. "There is absolutely no way I'm giving birth in an elevator, so just forget it. In fact, I've decided I'm not doing this. Not here, not ever."

"Daphne—"

"Get those paramedics," Daphne snarled. "Because if I can't have this baby in a hospital, I'm not having it at all."

Sam opened her mouth but the next contraction hit and she had to make a grab for Daphne before the girl hit the floor. Once it passed, Sam sank onto the floor beside her and stared at the hunky doctor.

Adam, she reminded herself. His name was Adam and he had one knee on the floor, his large hands on Daphne's belly. The look of concentration on his handsome face was surprisingly attractive.

"Are you okay, Daph?" Her heart was racing and she felt the edge of hysteria trying to push through her shaky control.

Oh, God. She hoped the EMTs made it in time.

"No. I…am…not…okay," the other woman gritted out, as she dug her fingers into Sam's arm and rode the next wave by huffing, puffing and squeezing out a strangled moan. "I'm about to pass a watermelon through my vagina. What part of that sounds okay?"

Sam winced again, both because Daphne's grip rivaled a muscle-bound logger and she had used the *V* word in the presence of a man neither of them knew—even if he *was* a doctor.

"You're going to be fine," Adam said, a hint of warm laughter in his voice that he quickly swallowed the instant two outraged females turned to glare at him.

Daphne huffed and puffed, eyeing him with intense dislike. "This is all your fault," she snarled through gritted teeth.

A dark eyebrow climbed up his tanned forehead as he eyed her warily. "Me?"

"You're a guy, right?" Daphne snapped, suddenly collapsing against Sam and breathing like she'd run up twelve flights of stairs in stilettos. She pointed a shaky finger at Adam. "If you and your...your *kind* didn't look at women with those hot, sexy eyes, none of this would happen." Sam assumed by the way she said *your kind*—bitten off with more than an edge of teeth—that she was contemplating violence against poor old Stan.

"Look at him," the girl panted, glaring at Adam. "I just bet he could impregnate some unsuspecting woman at a hundred paces. Better watch those eyes, girl. They're *potent*. One look and he'll have you performing a naked lap dance."

Sam made a strangled sound in the back of her throat and snapped her knees together as though Daphne knew what she'd been up to a couple hours earlier. And as though *he* knew what she was thinking, Adam's amusement grew, his warm gaze snaring hers and holding it captive as his grin widened.

Just when she thought things couldn't get any worse, she heard Adam say, "Can you remove her underwear so I can check dilation?"

Blinking at him uncertainly, she said, "I'm

sure you didn't mean what I think you just said because there's no way I'm removing *anyone's* underwear. Let alone someone I only met two days ago."

"*Hey*," Daphne objected through clenched teeth. "We survived two days of the high school histrionics together, so I think we're more than a little acquainted."

Adam's eyes were clear with a message she had no trouble interpreting. His expression said that if he'd asked her to remove *her* panties, she wouldn't have been balking.

Okay, so he might be right. *Maybe*. But she'd need another dozen shooters to contemplate that.

"Oh, for God's sake," Daphne burst out. "It's not like he's going to be seeing *your* lady parts stretched beyond recognition. I'd do it myself but—*Oh, God*!" She squinted at Adam in panic and sprawled onto her back to huff and pant like she was struggling for air. "Tell me they're not getting closer together because I told you we're not doing this here."

"Okay," he said mildly, sending Sam a pointed look. "I won't, but it would help if I could see what's going on."

Sam hesitated for a couple of beats, then sighed in resignation because no amount of pretending was going to change the situation. Besides, she was almost twenty-eight. Practically thirty. Way past the age when she should be over a stupid little thing like embarrassment and panic attacks at the worst possible moment.

Reaching beneath Daphne's bridesmaid dress—the one that made the pregnant woman look like a giant luminous beach ball decked out in a frilly pink skirt, she felt for the hip band and gave a tug.

Apparently enjoying her discomfort, Daphne giggled and tried to lift her heaving body off the floor so Sam could tug her underwear down her thighs. Too busy trying to pretend Adam wasn't controlling a smile and or that she removed people's underwear every day, Sam ended up wrestling with it like a demented squirrel digging for nuts when the swatch of lace snagged on Daphne's two-inch heel.

Oh, God. Face flaming and muttering something about guys being useful for exactly nothing except turning women into giant beach balls with legs, she yanked at the offending garment and shoved it at a giggling Daphne.

Adam was silent for a couple of beats, then said mildly, "Good job," with such a straight face that Daphne's hoot of hilarity smoothed over his next move as he gently nudged her knees apart and bent to look at ground zero.

With perspiration dotting her brow and seeming unconcerned that a man other than Stanley was looking at her naked crotch, Daphne huffed out breathlessly, "Tell me you were mistaken and that I'm not about to—oh," and promptly broke off with a low moan as another contraction hit.

"No mistaking that, Daph," Adam said quietly, sending Sam a narrow-eyed look. "Junior's head is already crowning. Don't push until I say, okay?"

"I thought I told you we weren't doing this here," the laboring woman wheezed as she collapsed against Sam. "Besides, I want to push more than *anything*. Except maybe strangle Stan for getting me this way." Then she grabbed Sam's hand and squeezed as she rode out the next contraction. "And the instant I get out of here," she gritted out, "I'm telling him there'll be no more sex for him…*ever*!"

"Okay, Daphne," Adam said calmly, his eyes gleaming with concentration. "The head's emerging. I want you to push now."

Daphne's body bowed with the force of her effort and her face went red until Sam thought she'd pop a blood vessel. She made a godawful noise that sounded like she was being ripped apart from the inside and Sam's heart clutched in sympathy.

She locked her gaze on Adam's face, the calm in the storm. But—what if something went wrong, she thought suddenly. What if the baby got stuck and they couldn't get it out? Her heart stuttered, a fist closing around her chest in a squeezing grip that threatened to cut off her air because she suddenly wanted more than anything to help.

Her fingers went numb and there was a loud buzzing in her head. What if…what if she froze and Daphne—or her baby—died because Sam was too terrified to move? What if—?

"*Amanda*." A deep masculine voice penetrated the white noise blocking out everything but the tumble of memories that still managed to give her nightmares. Memories that still made her freeze nearly two decades later—

"Hey," Adam said, his voice deep and smooth and soothing.

Sam blinked, realizing that he was talking to her. "Huh?"

He waited until her gaze cleared. "You okay?"

Hiding a wince, she licked her dry lips. "I'm f-fine," she said with grim determination. *Get a grip*, she ordered herself. *It's not like you're the one giving birth*. "I've just never w-witnessed a b-birth before."

After a short silence, he nodded. "It'll be okay," he said briskly, straightening to pull off his jacket. "Women have been giving birth for millennia." She only just prevented the jacket from slapping her in the face when he tossed it at her. She opened her mouth to ask what the heck he was doing when he reached between his shoulder blades with one hand and proceeded to strip his T-shirt over his head in that unique way guys had of undressing, leaving her gaping at him in shock—and admiration, darn it.

"Damn," Daphne wheezed, echoing Sam's thoughts and staring at a whole symphony of muscles bunching and flexing beneath acres of satin-smooth skin. "I'd hate you if you weren't so pretty to look at."

And because Sam was staring at him, she'd swear she detected a rush of color beneath his skin. She blinked. *Had the hot guy just blushed?*

Without missing a beat, he ordered, "Another push, Daph," sending Sam a challenging stare as he thrust his T-shirt at her. "Here, hold this. I'd ask you to sacrifice that dress for what's coming next but I have a feeling you're not wearing a hell of a lot under there."

Sam took the warm soft garment and couldn't resist one last peek at his wide rippling chest, shifting arm muscles and sculpted abs covered in acres of dark coppery gold skin. The perfect distraction from the panic attack hovering at the edges of her mind. But even as her heartrate slowed, he was suddenly frowning and ordering Daphne to stop pushing.

"Stop?" the woman gasped, lifting her head to gape at him. "Are you crazy?" She let rip with an eerie moan that streaked up Sam's spine and set all her hair standing on end. "I can't stop now!"

"The cord," Adam said softly, doing something between Daphne's thighs that Sam couldn't see. "It's wrapped around the baby's neck." He looked up briefly as both women inhaled sharply. "But not to worry," he soothed, transferring his attention back to what he was doing. "As long as you don't push or put pressure on this…" He cursed softly which made Sam's blood run cold and then he was humming encouragement. "Got it. All clear. Just a couple more pushes, Daph, and you'll be able to hold your baby."

By the time they heard the commotion and a frantic man yelling, "Daphne, I'm coming, babe," Daphne was propped up against Sam, gazing with wide-eyed wonder at the miracle in her arms.

Fifteen minutes later, the elevator had reached the lobby and the paramedics were rushing forward to take over the care of Daphne and her baby.

Trembling from reaction, Sam would have tripped in her haste to get out of the elevator if not for the large warm hand cupping her elbow and keeping her upright.

"Don't go anywhere," Adam murmured in her ear, as he brushed past her to where the EMTs were loading Daphne onto the waiting stretcher. The look of utter pride and joy on Stan's face as he stared down at his wife and child brought tears to Sam's eyes. Thank God Adam had been there to prevent Daphne's baby from strangling himself on his umbilical. Thank God *she* hadn't let Daphne down, she thought as relief washed over her in a knee-weakening rush. And thank God she'd kept herself from losing it. It had been a close call, but other than those brief moments of mind-numbing panic, she'd managed to breathe through the worst of it and help bring a child into the world.

That in itself was a major victory but—

Daphne's sharp, "Wait!" cut through Sam's thoughts and she looked up to see the other woman staring at her. "I don't know how much to thank you for being there. I hope you don't mind."

Sam blinked in confusion. "Mind?"

Looking flushed and serene, Daph linked her fingers with Stan's and leaned into him. "That I named him after you both." She looked briefly up at Stan, who nodded. "Meet Samuel Adam Prescott."

Stunned, Sam could only stare back and manage a garbled, "It's… I… I didn't do anything, Daph. I—"

"You did," Daphne interrupted huskily. "More than you know."

Sam gulped, terrified that she would lose control of the threatening tears "You're w-welcome," she rasped.

Adam, who must have realized that she was holding onto her composure with difficulty said, "It's an honor, Daph and she's right, we didn't do anything. You did all the hard work."

His deep baritone poured over Sam like warm honey, making her feel as though they'd been partners when she knew he'd been the center of calm.

"I know I acted like a crazy person in there," Daphne continued solemnly, echoing Sam's thoughts. "But I was wrong."

Sam licked her dry lips. "W-wrong?" God knows Sam was starting to sound like a parrot but she couldn't seem to help herself. The combination of adrenaline, a very private sense of accomplishment and the solid male strength and heat seeping into her back had rendered her speechless.

Daphne smirked at Adam's close proximity to Sam. "So totally worth it," she said, waggling her eyebrows. "Even from a hundred paces." She was grinning broadly as they wheeled her away, leaving Sam burning with embarrassment because

Adam, who knew exactly what Daphne meant, chuckled softly in her ear.

Her body responded instantly, her skin hot and itchy suddenly felt two sizes too small for her body. Like her hormones were suddenly in overdrive.

What the heck, she thought, aghast. What normal woman emerged from a crisis feeling jittery and turned on enough to contemplate jumping a complete stranger?

Clearly, she needed to get out of there before she did something reckless and crazy.

CHAPTER THREE

ADAM LOOKED DOWN into Amanda's face, noting her high color and ragged breathing.

"You okay?" he asked softly.

She jolted like he'd zapped her with a live current. Nervously licking her lips, she lifted her eyes briefly to his, only to skitter away again at the intensity she found there.

"Uh, excuse me?"

"You're flushed and jumpy."

Her flush promptly deepened, making him wish he could read her mind. Avoiding his gaze, she lifted a hand to fan her face. "It's really hot in here," she said breathlessly, blithely ignoring the blast of cool air from the overhead air vent and the wash of goose bumps popping out across her skin. "I think I'm having a coronary. Maybe I should have it checked out."

"You're not having a coronary," Adam said calmly, having seen her dilated pupils and the rapid pulse in her throat.

She sucked in air and pressed the heel of her hand to her breastbone. "Are you sure? It feels like I'm having a heart attack."

"You're having a panic attack." The panic—coming on the heels of her bold kiss in the bar earlier—came as a surprise. He'd have pegged her as a party girl if not for the fear he'd seen beneath her pale-faced determination to handle a potential crisis and the way she was currently clutching his jacket as though her life depended on it.

Her eyes cut to him, eyelashes fluttering wildly. "Don't be ridiculous. I am not panicking."

"All right," he said reasonably. "Then tell me that wildly fluttering pulse in your throat is a sign of arousal." One hand flew to her throat. "That your hand is shaking because you want to touch me and your ragged breathing is a sign that you want to be kissed…and touched."

Her eyes widened. "What? *N-no!*" she choked out and spun away, her eyes darting around as though searching for an escape route. He stepped into her and caught her shoulders in his hands, forcing her gaze to his.

"Then maybe," he said gently, shamelessly using his soothing doctor voice, "you should tell me what has you so spooked that you're considering bolting out into the night. Which I would advise against," he said when her gaze flickered in the direction of the street while her body vibrated like a guitar string. "Not in that dress."

Her eyes flew back to his and after a couple of beats, her shoulders sagged, her eyes squeezing shut. She abruptly turned away but he'd already seen her face and could only wonder at the embarrassed misery. Something moved in him then—something hot and tight and unfamiliar. Something that stirred that strange feeling of connection.

Hating to see her suffer, Adam tugged her around and dipped his knees to peer into her face. "Hey." He gave a gentle shake. "It's not that bad."

"Not for you, maybe," she hiccupped on a shaky laugh. "You're not the one who looks like a neurotic flamingo."

"A very cute flamingo," he chuckled, relieved to see the panic fading from her gorgeous eyes. "And everyone has a neurosis or two."

She took a deep breath that threatened the integrity of her bodice, briefly drawing Adam's fascinated gaze. "I bet you don't," she said, releasing her indrawn breath in a long sigh. "I bet you don't let the past freeze you at the wrong moment so that you're useless."

Adam studied her a long moment, wondering what had happened in her past that sent her into panic mode at the hint of an emergency. "You'd be wrong," he said mildly. "I have my demons the same as anyone else."

He could see by her expression that he'd caught her interest. "I bet you don't let it turn you into a shaking mass of insecurities though," she pointed out with a touch of self-loathing.

"Don't be so hard on yourself," Adam chastised gently. "I'm just better trained at handling medical emergencies." Feelings though? *They* usually sent him into a panic. Especially odd feelings for women in pink. Feelings that tempted him to sweep her into his arms so that he could provide the protection of a strong chest and broad shoulders.

Those—those were dangerous and to be avoided at all costs.

"I come from a family of doctors," she burst out in a low agitated voice like she was admitting some deep dark secret. "You'd think I would have learned enough not to freak out when someone goes into labor."

"Hey, *I* nearly panicked when she went into labor," he admitted with a chuckle. "I'm a cardiothoracic surgeon, not an ob-gyn. Heart attack? I'm your guy. But birthing babies?" He gave an exaggerated shudder. "Believe me, I panicked."

"You did not," she argued on a spluttered laugh. "You were great with Daphne." She paused for a long moment, her eyes searching his face. "You're a great doctor."

"Yeah," he agreed so casually that she laughed again. His gaze warmed. "At least that got you to stop thinking about whatever it was that had you wanting to bolt for the door."

For an instant, she seemed startled, then her eyes narrowed speculatively. "Hmmm, you're sneaky too," she muttered and turned blindly, reaching out a slender arm to call an elevator and froze for one pulse beat. Snatching her hand away, she turned in one jerky move, her eyes huge as they met his. "Do you think—?"

"It's probably safe," he said calmly, correctly interpreting her wide-eyed hesitation. "What are the chances of it happening twice in one night, right?"

She backed up a couple of steps, looking alarmed. "Don't say that."

"Why?"

"It's tempting fate." His amusement about tempting fate grew, when he'd all but accepted it.

"Would it help if I joined you?" he asked casually, leaning forward to press the button she'd avoided like it might bite.

Her eyes widened. "I, uh—"

The adjacent doors swished open and after a visible struggle, she drew in a deep breath but didn't move. Adam slapped a hand on the doors to keep them from closing and placed the other low on her back to usher her inside. He could tell by the abrupt tension vibrating through her that she was thinking about bailing.

"It's okay," he assured her when she reluctantly stepped inside. "Seems like they solved the problem." Her look was guarded as she brushed trembling fingers against her upper lip in a nervous gesture. His amusement faded at the sight of that quick tremble she ruthlessly squashed, and he shot out a hand to keep the doors open. "If you're worried, we can take the stairs."

Pursing her lips, she exhaled in an explosive burst that drew Adam's gaze to the generous pink mouth he knew from recent experience was soft and warm and sweet.

"Twenty-five floors?" She quickly shook her head. Shoving his jacket at him, she abruptly brushed his hand away from the touch pad, in a move he was certain was impulsive, and jabbed at her floor number.

The doors slid closed and the car began its silent ascent as Adam shrugged into his jacket. He'd have been blind not to notice the way her shoulders tensed, probably in anticipation of the elevator coming to another violent mid-floor stop.

Turning so that he was facing her, he breathed her in—coolly expensive with a hint of something hot and wild and tempting. Filling his lungs with her scent, he wondered who was the real her. Cool and classy—or hot and wild.

It would be interesting to find out because he had a feeling her cool, classy exterior hid a seething passion that was just waiting to burst free.

"I'm glad you were there to help Daphne," she said abruptly. "If it'd been up to me, we'd have been in serious trouble and—and I'd probably be missing a dress."

His mouth twitched at the image, but his eyes were intent when he told her quietly, "You don't give yourself enough credit. I think you'd have managed just fine."

"I faint at the sight of blood," she admitted baldly. "Pretty difficult to treat bleeding patients when your eyes are rolling back in your head."

He recalled her going pale at the idea of having to assist in an unexpected birth but despite that, there was intelligence and humor in those striking blue eyes along with a warm softness that drew him in.

He lifted a hand and gently brushed his thumb across her plump mouth. "You shouldn't let other people define who you are," he said firmly.

At first, she appeared startled by his words but her expression quickly turned thoughtful. After a short silence, she exhaled noisily and said shakily, "You're right. I shouldn't."

Before he could draw her out, the elevator dinged, announcing its arrival at his floor. "So," he said casually, reluctant to step out of the elevator and never see her again. "You want a nightcap?"

Sam knew he was offering more than a nightcap. To say she was tempted was an understatement, but the mention of her family had brought her back to reality with an unpleasant jolt.

"I—" She blew out a gusty breath. "I can't." Maybe circumstances—and a cheating fiancé— had brought her to a crossroads of sorts, but that didn't mean she was going to recklessly follow the urgings of her hormones.

Reckless would be pushing him up against the open door of the elevator and taking a bite out of his deliciously sculpted mouth. Reckless would be leaving the relative safety of the elevator with a man she'd spent a couple of intense hours with but didn't know from…well, from Adam.

And reckless would be taking him up on his invitation to a nightcap when she was already drunk on his pheromones.

Physically dragging herself back from that tempting edge, she wrapped her arms around her torso, locked her knees and stared at him helplessly. Oh, God. She wanted to. She really, *really* wanted to.

His eyes darkened seductively at her very obvious inner struggle. "You sure?"

His voice was quiet and deep, a little rough. Not demanding or aggressive, which would have instantly had her shields snapping into place. Despite the almost physical yearning rising up in her to say, *No, I'm not sure, take me anyway*, Sam found herself nodding and shaking her head at the same time.

Yikes. Way to be decisive.

Confused and tempted—so darn tempted, especially when disappointment flashed across his starkly handsome face—she bit her lip and nodded reluctantly.

Sending her one last searching look, he turned away and stepped forward as the doors opened. He was almost through the doorway when something inside her snapped. She gave a strangled gurgle that sounded like, "*Wait!*" And before she could reconsider, she was spinning Adam around and pushing him against the steel frame.

Sliding up against all that warm hardness, she rose onto her toes and for the second time that night, caught his mouth in an awkward, desperate kiss because she suddenly couldn't face the thought of him walking away.

Adam heard her swift intake of breath and had already half turned when she launched herself at him, filling his arms with warm curvy woman. He staggered back against the door, and in that instant, she had her arms around his neck and her mouth pressed to his.

Not about to question his luck, he hauled her closer and slanted his mouth more comfortably across hers. He murmured against her lips and traced the tip of his tongue along the seam, coaxing them open. In the next heartbeat, he was sliding his tongue against the length of hers, drinking in her throaty moans.

God, she tasted delicious, like sweet temptation and decadent sin; like shy eagerness and bold seduction—just as he remembered.

She squirmed, kissing him with more enthusiasm than skill. It didn't matter because in an instant he was rock hard, going from zero to a hundred like a kid having his first French kiss. He widened his stance and slid his hands to her hips, pulling her snugly into his erection in a move that left no doubt about what he wanted.

She uttered a soft moan of yearning and wriggled closer, her nails lightly scraping his scalp as she tunneled her fingers into his hair. A shudder rocked his control, leaving his skin buzzing and his temperature spiking on a wave of pure reckless need.

God, he groaned silently, smoothing his palms from her hips up the slender curve of her waist to the outside of her breasts. He couldn't ever recall wanting a woman with such fierceness before. His instinct was to strip her out of the pink dress and run his mouth all over that soft silky skin.

But first. "Amanda," he murmured, feathering his mouth along the firm line of her jaw to her ear. "Tell me you're sober. Tell me you want this, that you're sure?"

She arched her neck, the move inviting his mouth to explore the long line of her throat. "Sure?" she echoed breathlessly.

"About this," he rasped, planting little nipping kisses down her throat to her shoulder while brushing the outer curves of her breasts with his thumbs. She gasped—the hitch in her throat the sexiest thing he'd ever heard. Needing to hear the sound again, he moved back a couple of inches so he could see her face and did it again. A shudder moved through her.

"Don't stop," she pleaded softly, fisting his hair and tugging him closer.

With a growl, Adam caught her mouth, ramping up the heat. He fed her hot hungry kisses until his head buzzed and the soft sounds she made in the back of her throat threatened to blow the top off his head.

Something bumped against his back, pulling him briefly out of the haze sucking him under. It took him a couple of seconds to realize that the elevator door was trying to close. It roused him long enough to realize that they were standing in an elevator opening, behaving like horny teenagers. He tried to think about why that was significant but he was too busy chasing her mouth with his.

When the door bumped his back again, he broke the kiss and sucked in a harsh breath in the hopes that it would clear his head. Curling his hands around her thighs, he hiked her up and without being prompted, she wrapped her long legs around his waist.

He blinked to clear his eyes and lurched sideways, hoping he had enough strength to stay upright long enough to get to his suite. It took him a moment to orient himself before he staggered down the passage.

He was shaking by the time they arrived and had to press her up against the wall to fumble in his pockets for his key card. Panting and dodging her seeking mouth, her roaming hands, it took him a half-dozen shaky tries—and double the number of laughing curses—before the door finally clicked open.

Within seconds, he'd shoved it open, staggered inside and kicked it closed to push her up against the entrance wall. The next few seconds were a frenzy of hands as they shoved aside clothing.

Even before Adam found her zipper tab, she'd

pushed aside his jacket and her hands were slid-ing down his back, her nails scraping a line of fire to the base of his spine.

He cursed and tried to slow things down, but she seemed determined to strip him of his clothes as quickly as she was stripping him of his sanity. Pressing her against the wall, he took his hands off her long enough to shrug out of his jacket, not caring where it landed. Instantly her mouth and hands took greedily while he battled to keep them both upright.

"Amanda...honey," he panted when she sank her teeth into the muscle between his neck and shoulder. "Slow...down or—dammit." He grabbed her marauding hands and pinned them against the wall beside her head. "Stop. Or it'll be over before I can get you naked."

The sound of Amanda's name drew Samantha out of her sensual haze long enough to discover that she was in a strange hotel room about to have sex with a man she barely knew. The re-alization should have shocked her because Sa-mantha Jefferies wasn't the kind of woman to throw herself at strange men or try to climb their bodies.

She nearly told him her name then, but tonight she had rocked a pink-prom wedding dress, given a lap dance to a gorgeous stranger in a bar and kissed him like they were drowning and she was giving them the kiss of life.

Because that's what it felt like—only the other way around. It was as if kissing Adam had jolted her to life. It sounded corny, but at that moment she wasn't Samantha Jefferies, daughter of Vivienne and Edward Jefferies, and this didn't need to make sense. She was Amanda, the woman who ran from high society weddings to kiss hot guys in bars. The kind of woman who helped bring life into the world and the kind of woman who would wriggle against a man's erection and not react like she'd been goosed.

It was a heady feeling to think that here she could be anything she wanted. And deciding that what she wanted was to remain Amanda—for tonight, at least—she dropped her legs and slid suggestively down the front of a gorgeous guy who wanted her as much as she wanted him, hitting all her good spots along the way.

And by the rough sound of Adam's groan, she was hitting all of his too.

Powerful emotions swept through her and for the first time in her life, she understood feminine power. The kind that had men losing control. And suddenly she loved the idea of being the kind of woman capable of getting a man like him to lose control.

But she wanted more, a whole lot more, and

with a hungry sound in the back of her throat, she arched up and kissed him wildly, recklessly giving herself over to the feeling of being someone else.

He was by far the hottest man she'd ever met. Toned and sculpted, his shoulders and torso were a work of art. His skin, a lovely warm coppery gold that she wanted to lick up one side and down the other, was stretched over some pretty awesome muscles that bunched and flexed with his every move.

He had a genuine eight-pack, a flat hard belly that could have been sculpted by a master, the delicious ridges angling over his hip bones and drawing her gaze to where they disappeared into his waistband.

Delicious, she thought, feeling her eyes cross a little at the thought of tasting all that toasty skin, of tracing the happy trail with her tongue from his shallow belly button to where it disappeared into the low-slung waistband of his jeans.

And the hefty package beyond. Her mouth watered.

She'd like to trace beyond.

"Are we stopping?"

Only to admire the scenery.

She licked her lips as she made the return trip to his molten gaze. Sleepy and aroused, it sent a bolt of fear and pure lust through her, making something deep in her core clench with longing.

"No," she said, leaning forward to place a hesitant kiss on his heated skin. But that wasn't enough and before she knew it, she was sliding her tongue across the taut surface, sinking her teeth into his muscular neck and nibbling kisses over the well-defined ball of his shoulder.

She reveled in his harshly indrawn breath and muttered curses.

Lost in the salty, exotic taste of him, she shamelessly traced all that masculine perfection, delighting in the way his flesh rippled beneath her mouth. His hands were cupping her bottom again, kneading her flesh and ratcheting up the tension and heat.

Emboldened by his enthusiasm, she scored her nails lightly over his belly before reaching for the metal button on his jeans. Rock hard muscles jumped and jittered beneath the tight skin in concert to the pounding of her pulse. Her gaze followed the path her hands took, coming to a screeching halt when she discovered the long thick length of him straining the jeans' zipper.

"That looks uncomfortable," she said with a husky laugh. She shivered at the promise of that aggressive sign of arousal. She dipped her hand into the gaping waistband, her fingers brushing something broad and hard, yet surprisingly soft.

Even without looking, she knew the blunt tip of him was eagerly reaching for her touch.

It didn't seem possible but he was as turned on as she was. The thought sent a shiver of excitement easing up the length of her spine ahead of the rushing heat. Looking up, her gaze locked with his, the blaze of heat prompting her to smooth the pearly bead over his broad tight crown and then lift her thumb to her mouth in a bold move that surprised as much as it excited her. She'd never done anything so daring or suggestive before.

Had never wanted to.

When Adam's gaze flared hotter, a low, ragged curse torn from him, she was glad she had, especially as it sent a rush of heat between her thighs. The sight of his tight features and enlarged pupils made her forget for a fleeting moment that she'd been on a mission to make him lose control.

While she was drinking in the fierce arousal clearly etched on his handsome face, he had both her wrists captured above her head and was breathing like he'd run up the twenty-five flights of stairs from the lobby. A flush of arousal edged his high cheekbones, making his eyes glitter like a tiger's eye. The expression in them had her teetering on a very fine edge; an edge that he nearly shoved her over when he hooked his free hand beneath her knee and hiked it up, shoving his hips against her as he took her mouth in a hungry, urgent kiss.

Long fingers slipped beneath the narrow strip of lace at her hip and followed it to the tiny triangle of material at the apex of her thighs. Her gasp at the feel of his roughened fingers brushing her most intimate flesh turned into a squeak of surprise when one of those long thick fingers drove into her wet heat.

Everything in her clenched and she thought she might climax on the spot. Sam tore her mouth from his to suck in a ragged breath before she lost consciousness.

You can't pass out now, she thought frantically. *You haven't seen him naked yet. You haven't got to the good parts yet.*

Not giving her a moment to collect herself, Adam dipped his head, his mouth hot and damp on her neck, his teeth scoring a line of fire along the large tendon to the delicate skin beneath her ear.

Wordlessly, she clutched at him, tilting her head to the side to give him room to continue doing delicious things to her neck and even more delicious things to the tiny button of nerves between her legs that throbbed in time to her pounding heart.

Swept into a world that was all heat and sensation, Sam threw back her head with a ragged wail when he hiked her leg higher and bent to close his mouth over the tip of one breast. She was unaware that she was moving impatiently until the tip of her breast stretched and then popped free when he drew back.

He growled at her in a voice so low and indistinct that she was unable to distinguish separate words.

"Wh-what?"

"Can you reach my pocket?"

She blinked at him in confusion. "What?"

"Condom," he rasped, chest heaving and looking a little wild. "Now."

Feeling a little wild herself, Sam slid her hands into his back pockets and withdrew a leather wallet with hands that were suddenly all thumbs and impatient need. After a few aborted attempts, she opened it and found what she was looking for. Tossing the wallet aside, she shoved one corner of the foil package between her teeth and ripped.

In one swift move, Adam had swept aside her thong and freed himself from his jeans. Hoping she hadn't damaged the latex, she leaned back and reached for the impressive erection between them.

He snatched the condom from her and brushed her fingers aside. "Next time," he rasped, sheathing himself with a hand that shook. And before she could remind him that there wouldn't be a next time, he pulled her legs up and entered her in one long hard thrust.

Sam's body instantly arched as her inner muscles spasmed around the unfamiliar invasion. His breath whooshed out and he stilled, head thrown back, neck straining and muscles ironhard as he struggled with his runaway control. It was the most erotic thing she'd ever seen.

But then every thought was directed to where they were joined, to where he stretched her to the point of pain. He was huge, bigger than any man she'd ever seen, and while she hadn't had sex in nearly two years, she couldn't ever remember it feeling this good. Couldn't remember *feeling* this good.

Her breasts throbbed as flames licked across her skin, tightening her belly and clenching the muscles surrounding his erection. She'd never been so "in the moment" before that she was blind to everything but the way his body felt invading hers.

Finally, he began to move. Slowly, purposefully, with long slow withdrawals and heavy solid thrusts. Moaning, Sam arched, tilting her hips to take him more fully.

He groaned and thrust harder, deeper. Light exploded behind her eyes and a delicious chaos began to swirl in her belly, edging up the heat and sending ripples of electricity streaking across her skin. She clutched at him to keep from spinning off into deep dark space but with each solid thrust, he sent her spiraling higher and higher.

Just when she thought that she couldn't take more, he changed the angle and speed of his thrusts. The air was filled with heavy breathing, muttered encouragement, ragged curses and the sound of flesh striking flesh.

"Open your eyes, Amanda," he rasped in a tight, hoarse voice. "I want to see you when you come." Incapable of resisting his demand, her lashes fluttered up and she found herself staring helplessly into pools of molten black surrounded by a thin circle of burning gold.

His inky hair fell over his brow, swaying with each pounding thrust, and half concealing his fierce expression. It was the hottest, most erotic thing she'd ever seen and with the next downward thrust and grind of his hips, she went careening over the edge.

Her body arched in a desperate bow and the sound that tore from her throat might have mortified her if she'd been capable of thought. Lost in the fiery ecstasy of her own climax, Sam was only vaguely aware of Adam's pounding race to the finish, the forceful slamming of his hips against hers and finally—the low thrilling sound of his release.

CHAPTER FOUR

Two months later

SAM UNCLIPPED HER seat belt and reached for her phone. Fortunately, the past two months had been a whirlwind of activity that had kept her from thinking too much—about Lawrence, canceling her wedding and San Francisco.

During the day, at least. At night—well that was another story altogether, but she'd have to put that brief chapter behind her because there would be no more tall dark gorgeous strangers in her future.

She shivered, recalling the last time she'd been seated in a pressurized cabin. She'd spent the entire flight back to Boston alternately blushing, grinning like an idiot and then feeling aghast at what she'd done.

Heat rose up from the center of her body like a volcanic pipe of magma when she recalled that she'd bought a hot pink thong and slept with a hot gorgeous man she'd known for all of three hours.

Omigod. She'd slept with a complete stranger! She must be an awful person to have spent the night with a strange guy only a couple of days after breaking off her engagement to a man she'd known and loved for years. Although, it was clear she didn't know him *nearly* as well as she'd thought.

She was a trollop and she was headed for hell. Okay, so she was actually heading back to California, but according to her grandmother, it was one and the same. Especially after dropping the there-will-be-no-wedding bomb that had put her relative in an icy uproar. She didn't care. There was no way she'd ever consider living a lie like her grandmother.

Something had happened to her during that weekend and now there was no going back. In the space of three days, her life had changed irrevocably. She'd walked in on something she'd give her left kidney to unsee, and then in a fit of furious rebellion, she had entered an upscale lingerie boutique and bought her first thong—heck she'd splurged on an entire bagful of sexy stuff in an attempt to make herself feel like a desirable woman again.

She'd worn a short pink princess dress more suited to a high school senior and entered a bar for the first time in her life to escape the nause-atingly sweet, romantic wedding where she was the tallest *and* oldest bridesmaid. Oh, yeah, and to avoid Mr. Hands.

She'd tossed back shooters with names no self-respecting Boston debutante would contemplate let alone say and given a gorgeous guy a lap dance. Then because he'd looked like tempta-tion, in a sexy dark angel way with his whiskey eyes and potent mouth, she'd kissed him like he was the last man she would taste before the earth was destroyed by an asteroid.

And if that wasn't enough, she'd then been stuck in a lift with a woman who'd gone into labor and practically attacked the hotter-than-sizzling dark angel the moment they were alone.

Who the heck could ignore or top that as a life-changing experience?

It was no wonder she'd felt like a completely different person when she'd returned to Boston. She'd felt as though her entire world had shifted on its axis and she was in the wrong place and time. It was like she'd woken from a cryogenic state to a world that no longer seemed familiar, feeling trapped in a life and body that was meant for someone else.

Fortunately, Colleen Rutherford, her grand-father's mistress of almost forty years, had come to her rescue, offering Sam a job as Operations

Director of The Galahad Foundation. Okay, so the job offer had come about a year ago but since Sam had been engaged and planning her wedding at the time, she'd declined.

It had taken a particularly difficult encounter with her grandmother to finally push her over the edge. Summoned to lunch at the Mandarin Oriental, the formidable CEO of Gilford Pharmaceuticals had proceeded to lecture her about her duty to the Gilford name. She'd ordered Sam to get over her childish whining and get her wedding to Lawrence Winthrop the Third back on track.

The command had stunned her, although it shouldn't have since her grandmother had been content to live a forty-year lie all for the sake of appearances. Lilian had brushed aside Sam's objections, ignored her explanations and told her men cheated all the time and that she owed it to the Gilfords to make a good marriage since her mother had let the name down by marrying a Jefferies.

Realizing her objections were falling on deaf ears, Sam had listened politely, then returned to the art museum where she was the outreach coordinator and phoned Colleen "Coco" Rutherford to ask if the job offer was still on the table.

Upon being assured that it was, she'd promptly accepted, typed up a resignation letter and put her South End house on the market all in the space of one afternoon.

Now here she was, one month later, winging her way west to start a new life. Pity she couldn't leave behind the images that had been burned into her brain because now that she was finally motionless—and heading to the scene of her fall from grace—all she could think about was the night she'd spent with Adam. And while there would never be a repeat, she regretted not staying a little longer. Regretted sneaking out of his hotel room while he'd been in the shower. Because as liberating as her taste of rebellion had felt at the time, Sam wasn't really cut out for the guilt and panic of one-night stands with gorgeous strangers.

She'd woken sprawled naked across a queen-size bed, feeling wonderfully lethargic and decadently used. Then, in the space of two heartbeats, reality had struck and she'd freaked out. She had absolutely no experience with morning-after etiquette—and she knew a heck of a lot about etiquette thanks to her grandmother—so while he was in the shower, she'd scrambled off the rumpled bed that smelled like a combination of them both, almost landing flat on her face when she tripped over the tangled bedding.

Carefully avoiding the empty foil squares littering the floor like anti-personnel mines, she'd

gathered her pink dress and strappy heels—
there'd been no sign of the hot pink thong—and
bolted.

While nervous of her ability to handle all the
impulsive life changes that she'd made over the
past few weeks, she couldn't help the dizzying
relief and the feeling of lightness at having dis-
carded her old life. At having finally taken control.

Where she was going, no one cared about the
Boston Gilfords or that she was the awkward
underachiever in a family that made the Rock-
efellers and Oppenheimers look like a bunch of
slackers.

Feeling deliciously free for the first time in her
life, Sam opened a new document on her smart-
phone and typed *The Plan* in the heading. She
might be a late bloomer, she admitted, but she
was doing things differently this time. Instead
of letting other people orchestrate her life and
weigh her down with their expectations—and
disappointments—she was going to direct her
own destiny. And to do that she needed a plan.

Frowning in concentration, she began to type.

*No more engagements to "suitable" men at
least in Gilford terms
No more caving to familial pressure
No more trying to be someone I'm not*

*No more trying to hide my curves, hair or
unfeminine height
No more sedate, tasteful underwear or low-
heeled shoes
No more panic attacks
And definitely no more one-night stands
with hot dark angels*

She was going to take charge of her destiny.
Or die trying.

Adam leaned back in his chair and stifled a yawn
that was more boredom than fatigue, although
there was a large portion of the latter from spending the past ten hours in surgery. He was tired,
hungry and the last place he wanted to be was
in a meeting at—he surreptitiously checked his
cell phone—8:00 p.m. on a Tuesday night.

As a founding member of The Galahad Foundation, he was expected to attend board meetings
but tonight he was drifting while Dr. Rutherford
listed the virtues and accomplishments of the
foundation's newest operations director—who
was glaringly conspicuous by her absence.

He'd already heard all about Samantha Jefferies of Boston from Coco Rutherford, having
voted in favor of the new appointee a month ago.
As long as he could concentrate on the reason for
the foundation—consultations, transplants and

surgeries for people unable to afford the huge medical costs—he was happy for anyone to take over the running of it, especially someone more experienced and suited to the position than a bunch of overworked doctors.

Up until now, Coco Rutherford, mentor and boss, had taken on the day-to-day duties with the rest of them pitching in as needed. Adam was a busy surgeon and hated drafting letters, deciding what fundraiser to host next or organizing organ-donation drives. He hated having to decide who was more deserving of transplants or surgical procedures—there were just so damn many who needed them—and he loathed hospital policy and red tape that prevented them from doing more. That was Coco's forte.

Stifling another yawn, Adam ignored the cup of coffee cooling at his elbow and let his mind wander—right down the path it insisted on wandering every time he had two minutes to himself. Ever since the weekend he'd presented a paper at UCSF School of Medicine, he'd thought about his Peony. Despite their unspoken agreement that it was just a one-night stand, he'd found himself wondering where she was, why she'd left without saying goodbye and if he'd ever see her again.

After that first explosive encounter, he'd taken time to explore her long lush body and had noticed the pale band of flesh on her ring finger.

He'd wondered if she'd removed her rings to pretend she wasn't married, if she was recently divorced or wanted one last wild weekend fling before tying the knot with another man.

Maybe her leaving while he was in the shower was a good thing because he wasn't in the habit of sleeping with married women or being some engaged girl's last wild fling. He'd been the result of an engaged debutante's final rebellion and had spent his entire life not belonging in either his father's or his mother's worlds.

Although he didn't know if Amanda was from a rich and powerful family, he'd been pretty sure that he'd been her big rebellion against something. And yet he'd woken hoping to talk her into spending the day with him because he hadn't wanted to let her go.

He knew nothing about her except her first name and that she panicked in a crisis.

Oh, yeah, and she had a tiny velvety mole on the outer curve of her left breast where it met her ribs, sexy dimples at the base of her spine and that she was the most responsive woman he'd ever been with. He also knew her lips were soft and full and that she enjoyed kissing more than any woman he knew. And when she was aroused, her startling blue eyes darkened to cobalt. Just the memory of her biting her lip to hold back the throaty moans and sexy sighs she'd made when he'd taken his mouth on a torturous exploration of her body, made him shift uncomfortably in his seat.

Adam was just about to suggest they postpone meeting the new recruit when he became aware of voices coming from the outer office.

The hair on his arms and the back of his neck rose in premonition and he looked up from where he'd been doodling peonies just as the door was flung open and a feminine whirlwind entered in a cloud of familiar perfume and breathless apologies.

"I'm so sorry I'm late," she murmured huskily, sliding into the nearest available seat—which just happened to be directly opposite Adam. "My flight was delayed in Boston and then the airline lost my luggage."

Everything inside him came to a screeching halt and he missed the rest of what she was saying, what Coco Rutherford said, as well as the murmurs from other board members. He missed everything because there in the flesh was the very woman he'd just been thinking about.

Or was it?

His gaze sharpened as he studied the newcomer, because although she bore a striking resemblance to the woman he'd spent a passionate night with, this woman looked more like an elegantly cool and well-put-together professional and less like his wild, flushed Peony.

Gone was the tousled hair and short pink princess dress and in its place was a just-above-the-knee wraparound turquoise dress edged with black piping that molded to her body and drew attention to the spectacular curves beneath. Her chestnut hair had been drawn back into a severe bun that showcased her startling blue eyes and creamy complexion. Her makeup was perfect despite the long flight delays and the frustration of missing luggage. Her lips were a soft pink and those long, long legs that ended in sexy black sling-backs, brought back some very pleasant memories.

Adam heard a loud buzzing in his ears and completely missed Coco's introductions to the rest of the board members.

If he'd wondered whether there were two women in the world who could look and sound exactly the same, down to a familiar soft gasp and the hint of a dimple in her right cheek, the moment he met those wide shocked blue eyes, he knew this cool, put-together stranger and his passionate, rumpled Peony were one and the same.

Rising languidly, he leaned across the table to offer his hand, forcing her to take it or appear rude. Her skin was cool as she slid her hand into his and he had to admire her game face, because even as he felt the little jolt move through her, she didn't pull away. He knew she wanted to. It was there in her eyes.

He held on a little longer than was polite, and when her eyes gave the barest flicker and she tugged on her hand, he let his mouth curve before releasing her.

"So it's… *Samantha*?" he asked politely, deliberately trailing his fingertips over her wrist and across her palm, his gaze dropping to where her fingers curled into the palm he'd just caressed. She blinked, and for just a second appeared too flustered to speak.

She finally gave a jerky nod. "That's right," she murmured, quickly turning away to face Coco whose speculative gaze was bouncing between them. That shiver of premonition he'd felt earlier was nothing to the one that moved through him now. It was as if Coco had caught the abrupt tension and was amused and oddly pleased by it. Sitting back, he folded his arms across his chest to stare at his mentor in silent challenge. Her reply was an arched brow and a quick grin before she went back to addressing the meeting.

Adam pretended to listen but heard nothing. He was too busy watching out of the corner of his eyes as Samantha pretended he didn't exist. He knew it was a pretense because he caught her sneaking peeks at him when she thought no one was looking. He could practically see the tension shimmering off her body.

Hugely enjoying himself, he turned his head and let their gazes lock. He didn't know what she saw in his expression but she quickly looked away, picked up the folder containing the latest financial report and fanned her flushed face.

Finally, when Coco announced that the meeting was closed and invited everyone for refreshments, the room cleared of all but Adam and Coco in less than a minute. Slowly shoving back from the table, he followed Samantha's quick escape with his eyes. He wanted answers. But first things first, he thought, as Coco picked up her cell phone to either check her emails or to pretend she was in an effort to discourage conversation. However, Adam had known her since she'd elected to be his med school mentor and he wasn't easily put off. "What are you up to?" he asked when they were alone.

She lifted a finger in a brief give-me-a-minute gesture, then continued to tap away before finally lifting her head. Her expression was coolly enquiring but Adam caught a glint in her gray eyes, as well as the quickly suppressed smile at the corners of her mouth.

"I have no idea what you're talking about, Dr. Knight. Perhaps you could be more specific."

"I'm talking about that look," he said, jabbing a finger in her direction. "And the fact that I've known you long enough to know when you're up to something. Why do I have the feeling the other shoe is about to drop?"

Coco chuckled. "You're getting paranoid, my dear boy. Perhaps you've been working too hard. Come," she said, rising from the table. "You look hungry and I know you must be dying to talk to Sammie."

Geez, was he so damned transparent? "I am?"

"Of course you are." A smirk flashed across her face. "She has a million ideas for fundraisers that are bound to make us a lot of money."

He narrowed his eyes as she swept from the room, leaving him to follow. *Yep*, he decided, she was definitely up to something. And yep, he *was* dying to talk to *Sammie*, but not about her fundraising ideas. First, he was going to ask why the groomsman had called her Amanda— he'd neglected to ask, having better things to focus on during that heated night they shared— and then he was going to—heck, he didn't know what, he thought with a buzz of frustration. He only knew that all he could think about was undoing those four large buttons holding her dress together and sliding his hands up her smooth thighs. He wanted to taste her mouth to see if it was as sweet as he remembered and maybe muss her up a little.

Okay, he decided when his gaze instantly found her laughing at something someone had said, so maybe he wanted to muss her up a lot. He wanted to get her alone and put his mouth on that spot beneath her ear that gave her a full body shiver and hear her breath catch in her throat.

For the next half hour, Adam pretended to enjoy the food and conversation as he stalked Samantha around the room. He'd casually work his way to the group she was with and watch in amusement as she quietly excused herself. Just as he was beginning to lose interest in the game, she murmured something to Coco and slipped from the room.

Taking it as his cue, he followed, catching sight of a flash of turquoise as he got to the door. By the time he pushed through the outer suite door, the ladies' bathroom door halfway down the passage was closing, telling him where she'd disappeared.

After a quick over-the-shoulder glance to make certain they were alone, he followed.

Sam stumbled into the ladies' room and collapsed against the rich cream-and-sage-green wall. Gulping air, she pressed a shaky hand to the awful cramping in her belly. *Oh, God, oh,*

God, oh, God. The man she'd spent a reckless night having hot sex with in San Francisco was an executive member of the foundation she was now running—*in San José.*

Granted, the two cities were close, but never in her wildest dreams—fine, nightmares, she corrected a little hysterically—had she thought she'd see him again.

She squeezed her eyes closed, hoping that when she opened them everything would be back to normal because this was the worst thing that could have happened. She was supposed to be starting over with a clean slate and having her past come back to bite her in the ass wasn't part of her pla—

"Running away again, *Amanda*?" a deep voice asked quietly.

CHAPTER FIVE

SAM JUMPED SO high she was surprised she didn't give herself a concussion on the ceiling. Her eyes flew open to where Adam leaned against the door a few feet away. Hands thrust into the pockets of his black scrub pants, he looked casual and relaxed. She hadn't heard him enter, but then again the entire fifth battalion could have entered guns blazing and she wouldn't have heard anything over the wave of panic rushing over her.

She lifted a shaky hand to press against her racing heart and hoped he couldn't hear it flopping around in her chest. "I have no idea what you're talking about."

Despite her denial, memories of the night they'd spent together assaulted her and she suddenly wanted to thrust her hands into all that cool black hair and pull his mouth to hers. Or maybe slide them beneath his black scrub top so she could feel those fabulous satin-covered abs.

Aghast that she was imagining stripping him

naked, Sam stayed where she was and eyed him warily. He looked even better than she remembered and that bothered her because she'd remembered plenty.

For long moments, they studied each other until Sam pushed away from the wall, annoyed that she was letting old insecurities surface. She went straight to the vanity counter, hoping the distance would clear her head.

"My name is Samantha."

One dark brow arched up his tanned forehead. "Uh-huh and was that just for the benefit of the board members or are you really going to pretend we haven't met? That you have a twin somewhere in Frisco who looks exactly like you," he murmured, his eyes sliding across her face. "Right down to the freckles sprinkled across your nose?"

"Freckles?" she gasped in outrage, totally forgetting that she'd decided to pretend they'd never met. "I do not have any freckles."

"Wanna bet?" he challenged softly. "There are fourteen across your nose, five on your—" His gaze dropped to the reflection of her breasts in the mirror, causing the breath to back up in her lungs when her nipples tightened. "A dozen scattered down your back and three on the inside of your right thigh." He reached out to run a teasing finger slowly, tortuously, down the length of her spine, scattering her senses and sending goose bumps stampeding across her skin, racing down the center of her back to the base of her spine. "I know," he murmured wickedly, "because I tasted every one of them."

Heat spread outward at the careless sensuality of that caress but she suppressed it. "N-not everyone is lucky enough to have s-skin that doesn't blemish in the sun," she managed to say through the rush of sensation.

He stilled, and for a moment she thought she'd offended him, but then he leaned forward to blow on her neck. And heck if her scalp didn't prickle along with the soles of her feet. For an instant, she wondered if her hair was smoldering, but a quick glance assured her she was still Samantha Jefferies, cool and elegantly professional.

Except for the wild flush staining her cheekbones, wide eyes and dilated pupils. *Oh, God*, she thought spinning around to avoid the truth staring back at her. But when she found him close enough to feel the heat pumping off him like a nuclear reactor, she wondered at the wisdom of the move because he was so close she could see each individual speck of gold glinting behind the thick fringe of sooty lashes that drooped over his shimmering eyes. Eyes that abruptly reminded her of a stalking lion.

Her pulse jolted, because that's exactly what

he'd been doing. All through the meeting, he'd watched her watching him, and once it was over, he'd subtly stalked her from one group to the next until the only thing left was to escape into the ladies' room.

"What are you doing here, Adam?" she demanded, attempting to infuse her voice with cool outrage and cursing inwardly when it emerged husky and breathless instead.

Amusement came and went in his expression, infuriating her because he was too close, too disturbing, too—*everything*. She lifted her hands to his chest, intending to push him back a couple of inches but it was like moving a boulder.

"This is the ladies' room," she pointed out, ignoring the heat seeping into her palms and spreading up her arms; ignoring the very basic need to spread her fingers and feel all those amazingly hard planes and dips. "And the last time I checked, you don't qualify."

"So," he murmured, taking advantage of their proximity to toy with her earring. "You admit there *was* a last time, that you were the woman in Room 2014 who used her tongue to—"

"*Stop!*" she interrupted on a breathless squeak when she recalled exactly what she'd been inspired to do. Dammit, she was never mixing shooters and champagne again because that was the only explanation for the things she'd done that night. "Okay, so maybe I let you um…think my name was Amanda, but only because I never expected to see you again and didn't think it mattered."

His eyes darkened. "You don't think it matters to a man that he knows the name he groans whilst buried deep inside of that woman's body?"

She felt her core shudder at the memory of him doing just that in a voice so deep and rough her body instantly heated and melted in anticipation. "I…um—it does?"

His hands dropped to her hips and he tugged her against him, the move—and the feel of his substantial erection—leaving her in no doubt about what he meant. "Why don't we put it to the test, hmm?" he murmured, dropping his head to feather his lips along the soft underside of her jaw.

A painful rush of yearning gripped her and she found herself curling her fingers into his scrubs, tilting her head back to give him room to explore. She'd only spent a few hours with him and yet the way he touched her, skated his mouth and tongue across her skin, seemed achingly familiar.

"I d-don't think this is such a good idea," she heard herself say, heard the soft moan and wondered at the war going on inside her; to climb all over him or push him away and see that he stayed there.

Her mind yelled at her to step away while her body urged her closer.

Horrified that she might do something reckless, like rip off his shirt and sink her teeth into some part of him, Sam shoved him back and scuttled out of reach. She spun around and automatically reached out to turn on the tap and dispense a blob of foam hand soap into her palm.

"I—uh, this isn't what I want," she said in a voice she didn't recognize as her own. It sounded husky and throaty, as if they were stretched out on a bed in the dark.

Rubbing her hands together to spread the foam, she cleared her throat, not daring to look at him in case he saw past the desperate attempt to appear professional and in control. Heck. How was she supposed to act with a man who in many ways knew her better than the man she'd been engaged to?

"I left Boston because I needed a change," she explained, rinsing her hands and turning to address his chest because she couldn't look him in the eye. After a couple of beats, he wordlessly pulled a length of paper-toweling from the dispenser and held it out. Not seeing any other option, she took it and began to dry her hands. "Coco offered me this job about a year ago but

I was um—occupied with other things at the time."

Dropping the damp mess into the trash, she leaned her hip against the counter and folded her arms beneath her breasts in a move she knew was defensive but hoped looked casual. Just being in the same room with him made her nervous and edgy, because she couldn't recall ever coming across a situation like this in her grandmother's etiquette book.

Grimacing inwardly, Sam finally lifted her head and forced herself to meet his hooded gaze. "Then something happened and—" Pausing, she bit her lip and let her gaze slide away from his. It was one thing to admit how hurt she was at the discovery that Lawrence had been satisfying *his* physical urges all the time he'd been preaching abstinence until the wedding night, and quite another to have the man she's supposed to spend the rest of her life with lie to her.

"San Francisco."

Lost in thought, it took Sam a few moments to mentally catch up with the conversation.

"What? Yes—no." She paused to breathe in, then exhaled in one long shuddery breath. "Partly," she admitted shakily, rubbing at the tension between her eyes. "I, uh, realized that I was trying to please too many people and it took certain um—" she paused and flushed as one dark brow rose up his forehead "—events," she said more briskly, straightening her spine and glaring at him. "Before, during and after that weekend to show me I needed a change." She paused to swipe her tongue across her bottom lip and smooth a loose curl off her forehead. "I, uh—I didn't intend to have a one…um…night stand with you…or anyone else, for that matter. I want—no, I *need* to make a success of this to prove to myself that moving wasn't a mistake."

"And you think everyone knowing we slept together will jeopardize that?"

He sounded so amused, damn him, that Sam narrowed her gaze. "Yes—no." She broke off and lifted her chin at the open skepticism in his gaze. "Maybe. I don't know, but as we'll be working together, I don't want to muddy the waters with um—" She broke off and sucked in an unsteady breath.

"Sex?"

It was only when her breath whooshed out that she realized she'd been holding it.

"Yes."

After a long silence, during which Sam had to force herself to hold his stare, Adam's gaze dropped to her mouth, scattering all her good intentions. Her lips tingled and parted, her breath hitching softly in her throat.

The air thickened and warmed, swirling

around them like a firestorm of sensation that she couldn't ignore no matter how much she wanted to. A warning buzzed through her the instant his gaze returned to hers. Sensuality curved his mouth and blazed in his amber gaze, all but hypnotizing her.

"Okay," he murmured, shifting closer in a move that had the warning buzzing louder. "I'll be the soul of discretion in public." He paused to let his words drift between them before continuing. "But in private—" he lifted a hand to toy with the large button above her left breast "—I have no intention of letting you forget anything."

Distracted by his proximity, it took her a moment to realize that he'd very sneakily issued a challenge while her body and mind were in meltdown.

Sucking in a shocked breath, she lurched backward, knocking his hand aside. "Excuse me?" she demanded, outraged. "There won't be anything *in private* and there certainly won't be a repeat of…of…" She broke off to blush and curse at the dark brow rising up his forehead. "Of whatever it is you're thinking about. I told you. I'm done living my life to please everyone else. From now on, I'm going to please myself. I've got a plan and—and you're not in it."

In an instant, his eyes went flat and his jaw hardened. On a roll, Sam waved her hand in his direction. "And don't give me that look," she snapped. "Because it has nothing to do with your...your—" She broke off abruptly, unsure how to explain without offending him.

"My what?" he drawled smoothly, a muscle ticking in his jaw. "The fact that you had a wild steamy night with a man whose skin is too dark to fit into your rarefied blue-blooded world?"

Her mouth dropped open at the bitterness in his tone and she had to blink past the hot tears burning the backs of her eyes at the implied insult. Pressing a hand to the painful tightening in her chest, she sucked in air that felt like ground glass. "You r-really think that? You think I s-slept with you because...because—" She ground to a halt and swallowed convulsively.

"It's exciting to have a reckless fling with someone from the wrong side of the tracks before heading off to marry someone from a more suitable family?" His brow arched up his forehead. "You wouldn't be the first, *Sam*."

"Well, I'm not the latest either," she snapped, incensed that he would accuse her of bigotry when he didn't even know her. "For your information, it has nothing to do with your ancestry and everything to do with the fact that I'm not looking for a relationship right now, especially with a *doctor*." She said the word like it was something offensive and turned to fling herself away from him. When he said nothing, she spun back around to find him staring at her incredulously.

"All this is because I'm a doctor?" he demanded skeptically. "You can't be serious."

"My entire family consists of doctors and surgeons," she said heatedly. "I was an unplanned late-in-life baby and spent my childhood wishing I had some mysteriously interesting medical condition that would get my parents to notice me. And don't smile," she fumed. "It was awful. I was foisted onto nannies, housekeepers and finally my grandmother who had as little time for me as my parents did."

She sucked in a steadying breath because the last thing she wanted was pity from anyone. Especially him.

"I used to think that I'd been abducted by aliens at birth and given to the wrong family, because that was the only explanation for the fact that I had no aptitude when it came to medicine and panicked at the sight of blood."

"Aliens?"

"My point *is*," she said, rolling her eyes in exasperation. "I get that doctors are driven to save people with their superpowers but I'm not interested in anyone determined to prove he's God's miracle worker. It's too—lonely."

"So you're what? Looking for a man who stays home and rubs your feet?"

"Who says I'm looking for a man at all?" she snapped, incensed.

Adam's eyes gleamed with amusement. "Seriously?" His mouth curved into a wicked smile. "After San Francisco, you're trying to sell me that?"

Sam felt her face heat and huffed out in annoyance. Trust a man to twist her words into something sexual. "I'm not trying to sell anything," she informed him primly. "I'm merely explaining why I'm not looking for a relationship right now. Besides, with my track record with men— look, it's nothing personal," she added hastily.

"Nothing personal, huh?" he demanded softly, his eyes gleaming a sensual warning that skittered down her spine. He gave a short laugh and propped his shoulder casually against the wall. "I'm not supposed to take it personally that I'm good enough for a hot night of rebellion against your family but nothing else?"

"I didn't sleep—" She gulped at the look on his face. Drawing in a shaky breath, she tried again. "I didn't have sex with you to get back at my family."

"Who then? Your husband? Your fiancé?"

Sam felt herself go pale. "Who—who told you I had a fiancé?" she demanded hoarsely. For several beats, Adam stared at her, then reached out and caught her left hand. She tried to pull away but he easily lifted it and turned her hand so her ring finger was visible.

"This," he said, indicating the pale band of flesh where Lawrence's ring had rested for two years. "Although that night the indentation left in your finger looked fresh. As though you'd recently removed your ring."

Powerless to deny the truth, Sam sagged against the wall and studied the differences between their hands; hers pale and delicate against the large dark masculinity of his. "I *had* recently removed it," she admitted softly, her gaze flying up when his fingers tightened. It was her turn to wrap her hand around his to prevent him pulling away. "But it's not what you think," she added hastily, suddenly hating that he thought the worst of her.

"And exactly what *do* I think, Samantha?" he growled, his gaze shuttered against her.

"That I slept with you while being engaged to another man." After a moment, one brow rose up his forehead in query. "I um—" She licked her lips nervously and tried to think but it was more difficult that she'd anticipated. Finally, unable to utter the words with his amber eyes watching her with the intent of an eagle poised for attack, she dropped his hand and slid away.

When she could breathe, she said, "I'd already broken it off two days before we met," over her shoulder without meeting his eyes.

"Why?"

The question jolted her around. "W-why?"

Propping his shoulder against the wall, he folded his arms across his chest. "Why did you break it off?"

Realizing that he probably deserved the truth, Sam blew out a breath. "I walked in on him and his—assistant having sex." He grimaced but said nothing. Goaded, she added, "His assistant's name is Ronnie, which is short for Ronald."

Understanding flickered in his gaze. "Oh."

"You got that right," she muttered and then sighed. "I felt—betrayed."

"Of course you did."

"No, you don't understand," she said heatedly, pushing her hair off her face. "I've known him forever. I believed him when he said he loved me. I thought he wanted to wait for the wedding night before we—um, before we—" She broke off, face heating with embarrassment when Adam's eyes narrowed.

"How long were you engaged?"

She finally muttered, "Almost two years," sighing with resignation when his eyebrows shot into his hairline.

"You were *celibate* for two years?"

She glared and folded her arms beneath her breasts, daring him to comment on her stupidity. "*I* was," she muttered. "*He,* however, wasn't."

His face was a mix of emotions that might have been comical if the situation weren't so mortifying. "Do you mean to tell me that night was your first time in two years?"

Her face flamed because it had been way longer than that. Embarrassed, annoyed and wishing she could escape, she set her jaw and demanded irritably, "What's that got to do with anything? I was just trying to explain why rebound sex is a bad idea and—"

"Have you heard of destiny?" he interrupted mildly.

She blinked, confused by the non sequitur. "Destiny?"

"Fate, providence, predestination, chance, karma or kismet, if you will."

"I know what it means," she said through clenched teeth. "I'm just not sure how it relates to this discussion."

He pushed away from the wall and stalked toward her until she found herself backed against the tiled wall. Annoyed that she'd allowed him to put her in retreat, Sam lifted her chin and met his gaze head-on.

"Did you know," he murmured, planting one hand flat against the wall beside her head, "that this is the fourth time we've been thrown together by *events*?"

"Events?"

"Yeah, you know destiny, fate."

She made a sound of annoyance. "There's no such thing. It was a coincidence."

"That we were in the same bar, in the same hotel at the same time? That you tumbled into *my* lap and not one of a dozen men surrounding the dance floor? That we decided to call it a night at the same time and ended up in the elevator together to help bring a child into the world? And then two months later, you cross the continent to work on the *same* foundation because we're both acquainted with Colleen Rutherford?" He paused to let his words sink in before leaning closer. "Not only don't I believe in coincidences, *Samantha*," he said softly, "there is no way I can ignore the fact that I already know you intimately."

Her throat moved convulsively as she swallowed. "You don't know a thing about me."

"Don't I?" he asked softly.

"That's just ph-physical stuff," she rasped, her body going hot at the reminder of how much he'd learned that night. "But that's beside the point. Rebound sex——"

"Is a bad idea," he interrupted roughly. "Yeah, I know. But here's the thing." He ran questing fingers up her arm, across her shoulder and down the neckline of her dress to where the two sides of her dress overlapped. "Rebound or not, I look at you and I can't forget."

"Well, I certainly won't have any problem forgetting anything," Sam lied, desperately ignoring the rush of sensation spreading out from the barely-there touch. "In fact, I'm really good at ignoring things that aren't good for me." For too long, she'd been really good at ignoring her own wants too, doing what was expected of a Gilford.

She pressed her hand against his chest in the hopes that he'd get the message and back off. "You're in the ladies' room. Now, please leave so I can get b-back to my p-plan."

Adam's eyes darkened and before she could squeak out a protest, he gently pulled her against him and brought his lips close enough to shock her into stillness and then strain for more. She yielded to temptation, slanting her lips against his and opening them to receive his invading tongue before she could remind herself that this was the last thing she wanted, that *he* was the last man she wanted.

But she did. Oh, God, she did. She'd wanted him in San Francisco and she'd wanted him while sitting across the boardroom table, pretending interest in what Aunt Coco was saying. She hadn't heard a thing over the panicked embarrassment and excitement pounding through her blood.

She shouldn't be kissing him. But she was and she didn't want to stop. Oh, God, she thought as she closed her lips around his tongue and sucked it into her mouth. She didn't want to stop the wild recklessness rising within her to give and take and then take some more.

And then, just as the edges of her vision grayed, he broke off the kiss with a ragged curse and backed away, leaving Sam clutching the vanity counter. Opening heavy eyes, she stared at him in confusion. He was half a dozen feet away, dragging air into his heaving lungs. After a slow burning stare, Adam turned and pulled open the door.

"Ignore *that*, if you can, Ms. Jefferies," he growled over his shoulder in a voice that was hardly recognizable, and then he was gone.

CHAPTER SIX

"Suction," Adam said, pausing to allow the surgical nurse to remove the blood pooling in the chest cavity. "Release the clamp and test the vessel for integrity," he instructed the surgical intern. "When you're certain the graft will hold, we can proceed with closure."

Satisfied that the young surgeon was coping, he looked up at the real-time image on the fluoroscope screen. So far, he couldn't detect any leaks. The new bypass seemed to be holding steady but the next forty-eight hours would be critical.

Out of the corner of his eye, he caught sight of movement in the observation window overlooking the surgical suite and turned as a figure rushed from the room. He didn't need to see her face to know who it was. That straight-as-a-ruler back and the warm fire of upswept chestnut hair gave her away.

His skull tightened and a tingle worked its way

down his spine. Since the foundation meeting a fortnight ago, giving Samantha the space she'd wanted had been both easier and more difficult than he'd imagined. Easier because there'd suddenly been a spate of new patients and he hadn't had time to sleep let alone follow his instincts. Which was where the difficulty had come in.

Now that he knew the woman who'd dropped into his lap and shaken his world with her bright blue eyes and enthusiastic kisses was right here in San José, giving her space had been the last thing he'd wanted, especially with her habit of appearing in the observation room in the middle of intricate procedures.

If he were honest with himself, it had stung having her call what to him had been the best sex of his life a rebound mistake, and he'd reacted like a nerdy adolescent experiencing his first rejection.

"How's the temperature holding, Mr Davis?" he asked the perfusionist, deliberately pushing thoughts of Samantha from his mind. The assisting surgeon had released the clamp and there was a collective inhalation as all eyes went to the fluoroscopy monitor. He caught the thumbs-up as everyone watched blood fill the graft section, then flood the heart. After a couple of shudders, it settled into a sluggish rhythm.

"Vitals?"

"Holding steady." This from the anesthetist.

"All right then, bring the temp up, Mr. Davis. Dr. Guthrie, let's proceed with closure." He waited while the two halves of the sternum were brought together. "Talons ready?"

Six hours later, Adam left the elevator and headed down the passage toward the children's ward. Four-year-old Katie Ross had undergone an atrial septal repair that morning and he wanted to check on her before calling it a day.

Although the procedure was a relatively simple one requiring a transcatheter repair and a tiny device—folded up like an umbrella in the catheter tube—deployed and attached over the hole, she would need careful monitoring over the next few weeks to ensure it did not detach and cause an embolism. Despite the septal defect, the little girl was a bouncy, bright-eyed little imp and keeping her quiet was going to take some doing.

He paused to check the ward register, then moved past the nurses' station toward the wards, wondering why it was so quiet when the children's ward was usually filled with the wails of distressed children and the murmured reassurances of nurses and mothers.

He caught the sound of murmured tones spoken into the hushed, expectant silence followed by a chorus of childish gasps. A low familiar feminine laugh sent him spinning back nearly three months.

He paused in the doorway to Katie's room, finding a group of children, ranging from about three to nine, gathered around Katie's bed. Some were leaning against their mothers while others practically bounced up and down in their excitement as the story unfolded.

Nurses quietly checked their vitals and the person using different voices to bring the story alive for the wide-eyed audience was none other than the woman he'd spent way too much time thinking about.

Samantha Jefferies. Not looking as out of place as she might with her upswept hair and off-the-shoulder half-sleeved rose-colored dress more suited to a fancy ladies' luncheon than the children's ward. Snuggled in her lap was a small boy with messy dark hair and sleepy eyes. Adam watched as she absently smoothed the overlong strands off his forehead before turning the page and continuing the story.

Disinclined to draw attention to himself and break up the story hour holding the children spellbound, Adam propped his shoulder against the open doorway and watched the engrossed little faces while a husky voice brought the story to life.

He sensed someone come up behind him and

turned to see Janice Norman. The Paeds APRN arched her brow at him before turning her attention to the gathering around Katie's bed. "She's great, isn't she?"

Adam turned back to the scene, his expression neutral. Janice had been in San Francisco the night he and Samantha had met and wasn't anyone's fool. She'd spot a weakness a mile away and take unholy delight in needling him.

"Ms. Jefferies come here a lot?" he murmured casually.

"Usually about this time," she said absently. "And sometimes in the afternoons when the kids are restless. They love her. She's a natural, and her stories distract them from all the poking and prodding."

Adam scratched his jaw and wondered if Janice knew that his heart was pumping a little faster, that a buzz had started at the base of his spine and traveled all the way to the top of his head at the sound of that husky voice. A voice he recalled urging him on. *Don't stop*, she'd ordered, *Harder*, and then on a sexy little hitch, *Oh...oh...right there*.

Just the memory had his body hardening, and by the knowing little smirk on Janice's lips, she recognized Sam and wasn't about to pass up the opportunity to rag him.

"You know," she remarked idly after a couple of beats, confirming Adam's worst fears. "I can't help noticing how much she reminds me of someone." Having known her since his intern days, she knew him better than anyone and enjoyed making him squirm. Schooling his features, he just grunted even as Samantha finally looked up and noticed she had another audience member.

She stopped abruptly mid-sentence, her eyes widening as she stared at him for a couple of beats before flushing and looking away. But in that moment, Adam had seen both anxiety and vulnerability beneath the surprise. The vulnerability got to him in a place he hadn't expected. His chest. Or more specifically his heart. It clenched hard and all he could do was rub the heel of his hand against the sharp ache.

Dammit, he snarled silently. The last thing he needed was to feel anything for the woman who'd relegated him to a rebound mistake. Even if he'd never thought to see her again.

"So..." Janice said casually. "You and the Prom Queen, huh?" Without waiting for him to reply, she glared at him and demanded, "When were you going to tell me that the woman from the bar in San Francisco is related to Dr. Rutherford and working for the foundation?"

Amused by the censure in her tone, Adam shrugged because he hadn't wanted to talk about

Samantha with anyone. He wasn't sure why; what had happened between them was just too private to discuss. Even with friends.

"They're not actually related," he said absently, before hitting her with what he hoped was a look of male bafflement that he didn't for a minute think she bought. "I think the connection has something to do with her grandfather." He let his gaze drift over the yawning kids, then squinted at his watch. "It's a bit late for story time, don't you think?"

Narrowed eyes promising retribution, she growled and shoved past him, leaving Adam relieved that he'd narrowly escaped a grilling. The relief was short-lived, however, when his gaze drifted back to Samantha and their eyes locked again. Hers widened and darkened as wild color rushed beneath the creamy skin, making him wonder if she was remembering that night too.

But did her determination to ignore what he felt between them stem from the fact that he was a doctor; that she'd only recently broken off her engagement and didn't want to jump into a new relationship too quickly; or because of his background? Not that he was looking for a relationship, he assured himself. She wouldn't be the first woman to sleep with a man because of the thrill of the forbidden and she probably wouldn't be the last.

His own mother had treated his father as a temporary thrill while she sowed her wild, youthful oats before marrying a man worthy of her blue-blooded status. He'd often wondered if falling pregnant had been a way to rebel against the strictures of her family or if she'd just been young and stupid. Whatever it was, he'd ended up collateral damage and spent most of his life fighting the prejudice of having one foot not only in his mother's culture but in his father's too.

He had no desire to repeat his parents' mistakes or be anyone's rebellious one-night stand. He thought too much of himself for that. He'd had to work twice as hard to be given even half the respect other students or doctors expected as their right. He'd never minded the hard work since it had put him on Coco Rutherford's radar and helped him become a top cardiothoracic surgeon.

He certainly didn't need a curvy chestnut-haired woman reminding him of his childhood and making him feel as though he was always on the outside looking in. As though he was good enough for wild rebound sex but not for anything more open or long-term. He refused to yearn for scraps of attention the way his father had, finally hitting a spiral of depression and alcohol because some vain, shallow debutante had only wanted a quick thrill.

Reminding of a past he had no intention of repeating, Adam pushed away from the door frame, suddenly needing fresh air. He would come back later, he told himself as he left the ward. He'd return to check on Katie when the ward was quiet—when he could think past the urge to mess up Samantha's sophisticated perfection in an effort to find the warm sexy woman from San Francisco.

Pulse jumping, Sam saw Adam's eyes change—narrow and cool—before he turned and disappeared. It was as though he'd come to some decision that she knew should have relieved her, but didn't.

Oh, boy, it really didn't.

And with that realization, she sucked in a sharp breath and cringed as her thoughts tumbled one over the other inside her head. Had she—had she secretly *wanted* Adam to ignore what she'd said about rebound sex and not give her the space she'd said she needed?

Her belly bottomed out and a rush of heat washed over her at the images that popped into her mind. Oh, God, she had, she thought with horror. In some silly feminine part of her, she'd secretly hoped that he wouldn't be able to stay away. That he'd ambush her, push her up against the nearest wall and kiss her senseless.

Her lips tingled but she ignored it, because it made her a vain and shallow person who said one thing while meaning another because he was hot and buff and made her feel like a sexy, desirable woman. Which meant, *dammit*, that for all her talk of changing her life, changing *herself*, she was still not taking charge of anything.

Cringing at the knowledge that she was falling back on old habits, she dispensed a few hugs with a promise to be back the next day. A headache squeezing her forehead, she returned Janice Norman's greeting with a wan smile and headed for the exit, eager to escape the woman's speculative gaze.

It was only when she was alone in the elevator that she recognized the roiling emotions for what they were. Jealousy. She was jealous of the closeness she'd sensed between Adam and the head paediatric nurse.

And if that didn't make her a pathetic fool, she didn't know what did.

It should have been easy for Adam to put Ms. Boston Socialite firmly out of his mind. He'd learned early on that he couldn't control everything and then put all his energy into doing just that. He'd focused on acing high school and then med school, needing to prove to himself that he'd been awarded the Stanford scholarship because he deserved it.

He'd worked two jobs until Coco swept into his life, becoming much more than a mentor. She'd arranged for him to work at the hospital so he could focus on medicine and bullied him to eat properly. At first, he'd been too proud to accept her help, but she'd simply told him that she was protecting her investment. When he'd realized that helping him was helping her get over the death of someone she'd loved, he'd accepted—albeit reluctantly—then worked his ass off to prove she hadn't been wrong about him.

There'd been women, of course, but he'd never allowed anyone to become a distraction from what was important; and *that* was overcoming his past and becoming the best cardiothoracic surgeon on the West Coast.

He'd been perfectly happy with the status quo, seeking out women when the need arose, all the while focusing his energies on professional goals. Then he'd met *Amanda*, who'd turned out to be Coco's Sammie, and his focus had shattered.

Okay, maybe not shattered, but she'd jolted him out of the nice little groove his life had become and made him want something he hadn't let himself want in a very long time.

He wanted a connection.

Ironic as hell, considering the woman wanted nothing—except distance—from him. Even worse, he hadn't realized how much he'd come to look forward to seeing her in the surgical observation room until she stopped coming.

And damn if he didn't miss her.

He scowled at the thought. Damn the woman, and damn the effect she had on him.

Then, before he'd realized he'd come to the decision, he found himself heading to the floors housing the hospital's top management late the following Friday. He'd been on his rounds when an idea had popped into his head fully formed.

The best way to get Samantha out of his system, he decided, was to spend some time with her and see how she handled a day in Juniper Falls where he was due for his monthly outreach visit. It was where the foundation had been conceived—and where he'd grown up. He was hoping the differences in their upbringing would cure him of his growing obsession with a woman that was way out of his social league.

It was only when he saw Coco sitting in reception, frowning at the computer screen, that he realized how late it was. The only other illumination came from one corner lamp.

"Adam," Coco said when he opened the door. She looked surprised to see him. "Is something wrong?"

"No, I uh—" His mind went blank for a couple of beats before abruptly coming back online. "Nothing's wrong but I was looking for Samantha and only just realized how late it is."

Coco frowned and turned her attention back to the screen. "Sammie? Why?"

He thought about leaving but then firmed his jaw. *Dammit*, he wasn't that awkward kid he'd been at fifteen screwing himself up inside over the most popular girl in school. Giving in to the discomfort, he rubbed the back of his neck and said as casually as he could, "I'm flying out to Juniper Falls in the morning and thought she might like to see what Galahad is all about. She's been here over a month and aside from meeting some of our recipients, she knows next to nothing about the foundation."

"Great idea." She waved her arm to the passage that led to the offices before resuming her keyboard clacking. "Don't know why I didn't think of it myself." She paused and sent him a quick grimace. "You just missed her though. She went out to dinner on a—"

"Date?" he interrupted so sharply that Coco looked up, her expression oddly arresting. Embarrassed by his outburst he brushed it aside with, "Never mind," his brows drawing together over the unpleasant emotions tightening the back of his skull at the realization that while he hadn't had a date in—heck, he couldn't remember—Samantha was out to dinner.

He knew exactly what the emotion was but it had been at least twenty years since he'd felt it, and he couldn't understand why it was emerging now.

"Do you have her cell number? I need to get an early start."

Coco grabbed a small notepad off the receptionist's desk and scribbled something. She tore off the top sheet and thrust it at him.

"What time do you plan to leave?"

"About five, why?"

"Better pick her up at four thirty with hot, sweet coffee. She's not an easy morning person. Oh, and Adam—" She waited for him to meet her gaze and after a couple of beats said, "Give her a chance."

Confusion tightened his forehead. "What are you talking about?"

"Sammie isn't anything like your mother," she said gently, her eyes dark and soft with a compassion that he abruptly wished wasn't focused on him. *Dammit*, he wasn't some orphan.

"I know that—" he began irritably only to have Coco interrupt.

"Do you?" she drawled softly, one brow arching up her forehead as though he were a little dense.

Frustration grabbed him by the throat. "What's that supposed to mean?" He wanted to tell her to mind her own business but she'd been mother, mentor and friend to him when no one else had cared.

"It means I know you too well," she said gently, pushing away from the desk, a challenge gleaming in the eyes that locked with his. "It means that every relationship you've had since we met has been with social butterflies. Relationships that had an expiration date even before they started."

"That isn't relevant," he growled. "Besides, Samantha and I do not have a relationship outside of the foundation."

Coco clucked her disappointment. "Do you think I haven't seen the way you look at each other when you think no one is watching? You're interested, Adam, but you're so determined to paint all socialites with the same brush as your mother that you'll overlook the fact that Sammie is warm and generous and funny—absolutely nothing like those other women."

What could he say to that but, "This is for the foundation," before turning and walking away.

Of course, Coco had to have the last word but she let him get to the door before saying smugly, "Oh, and in case you wondered—she's interested too."

CHAPTER SEVEN

SAM BLINKED BLEARILY up at the man leaning casually against the wall outside her apartment, looking alert and rested like it wasn't the middle of the night. His eyes took a leisurely journey over her and by the time they returned to her face, a smile tugged at the corners of his mouth.

The expression in his gaze sent a buzz of sensation zinging through her, clearing away the last remnants of sleep. Wondering if she was still dreaming about seeing him, standing in the exact same spot and with the same predatory expression in his eyes, Sam shoved the wild tangle of hair off her face and rasped, "Adam?"

One dark brow arched and his eyes darkened. "Expecting someone else?"

Even in her befuddled state, she caught the bite in his words and wondered what the heck he was mad about. It wasn't like *she'd* arrived on *his* doorstep in the middle of the night, dragging him from a deep sleep, then looking at him like he'd committed some heinous crime.

Shaking her head to clear it, she inhaled, swearing she could smell coffee. She must be dreaming or maybe it was part of the same Adam hallucination? "What are you doing here?" she rasped.

He was silent a beat before saying, "Our field trip." And when she continued to stare at him, said, "You did get my message, didn't you? I tried calling but your phone was off."

"Wha—?" She inhaled, hoping the cool air would clear her head. It had been a while since she'd been this close to Adam and it was messing with her head. "Oh, right. Yes, I—" At his arched brow, she broke off. Her hand tightened on the doorknob and she exhaled with a whoosh. "Sorry, you'd better come in."

He narrowed his gaze but didn't move. "You alone?"

"What?" She scowled her confusion, and when he just looked at her, scrubbed a hand over her face and muttered, "I need caffeine. I can't think this early."

Stepping back, she blinked a large to-go cup from a local coffee outlet into being. At first, she thought it was an apparition until it was followed by a large male that smelled even better than the hot beverage. For a scary moment, she worried that she might be tempted to drag him inside and gulp him down.

"Earth to Samantha." He chuckled, waving the coffee beneath her nose, and she realized she'd gone a little glazed with lust. She licked her lips and hastily assured herself that it was for coffee. Definitely for coffee.

"Looking for this?"

"Um—yes?"

When she continued to stand there and drool, he chuckled and caught her hand to wrap her fingers around the large cup. Warmth instantly infused her palm and traveled up to the inside of her elbow before spreading to the rest of her in insidious waves of pleasure.

"Late night?"

There it was again, that edge suggesting he was annoyed with her. Her brow tightened in confusion but the heat of his hand around hers was kind of distracting. She'd forgotten how large his hands were with their wide palms and long strong fingers; and she'd forgotten how they could make her feel.

And that wasn't good, she decided, when a shudder accompanied the memory. "It's not the late night," she blurted out, a little freaked that he just had to show up and she turned into a woman who couldn't recall her name or that she had a plan. One who'd danced barefoot in a five-star hotel bar, tossed back shooters like a pro and then helped deliver a baby in an elevator. "It's y-you."

"Me?"

Oh, great, now she was stuttering and about to admit that after seeing his missed call and listening to his deep voice inviting her on a field trip for the foundation, she'd hardly slept. She'd wished he were inviting her because he wanted to spend time with her and not because he wanted her to meet people connected to the foundation.

When she had slept, it had been to dream some pretty hot stuff that made her blush just recalling it. No way would she tell him all that though. Especially not with the way he was acting.

Then again, he had brought coffee.

"Ignore me," she muttered. "My brain always struggles to wake up in the middle of the night." She let him guide the cup to her mouth. Forced to take a testing sip of hot, sweet brew, she felt her system shudder and was pretty sure it was the infusion of caffeine.

"It's nearly five," he murmured. His voice, a little rough around the edges, reminded her of the way he sounded when he was aroused. "We should go."

Fighting memories of San Francisco, Sam tightened her grip on the to-go mug and finally found the presence of mind to step back. It was more of a stumble but she couldn't think with him so close, not when he looked and smelled so good that she contemplated testing to see if he tasted better than coffee. She licked her lips, afraid that he did.

"Go…?" Her brow creased in confusion. "Oh—right," she said on a rush of air and gestured out the door. "Let's go then."

He didn't move, just rocked back on his heels, his hot eyes lightening until he was smiling.

"What?" Annoyance tugged at her brows. *Yeesh*, it was bad enough that she was expected to think before the sun was up and now she had to deal with his annoying masculine amusement.

Annoyance she promptly forgot when he gave her a slow down-up look, his eyes a little heated as they returned to hers. "Not that I'm complaining," he drawled huskily. "But you might want to dress first."

"Wha—?" Sam looked down and realized that she was in her skimpy pajamas and a light summer robe that left very little to the imagination. Heat rose into her cheeks because the cool early morning air had tightened her nipples into visible buds. "Oh, boy," she muttered, rolling her eyes and spinning away to hurry through the arch toward her bedroom, calling, "I'll be right back. Make yourself at home," over her shoulder.

She took the fastest shower on record and returned twenty minutes later wearing a dress that she'd bought at a little gem of a boutique she'd found close to the hospital. It was part of her new-me makeover, and she had no idea why she'd chosen to wear something so outrageously feminine today of all days.

Adam, leaning against the French doors that opened onto the complex's communal gardens and swimming pool, turned at the sound of her heels clicking on the tiled floor and stilled. For one horrifying moment, she thought she'd made a mistake in her choice of white flowing midi sundress covered with large scattered red camia. Then he moved and the expression in his eyes had wariness and awareness rolling over her like a tidal wave.

Abruptly self-conscious, she had to force herself not to back away as he neared. Lifting her chin defiantly, she dared him to comment on her appearance because *dammit*, she had to stop feeling as though she were constantly being judged and found wanting. She had to stop worrying what other people thought and start pleasing herself.

That was the reason for moving across the country, wasn't it? To move out from the shadow of her grandmother and find herself. Find her own mojo. Be her own person.

Besides, the dress, with its tiny capped sleeves,

form-fitting bodice and full skirt had pleased her the instant she'd seen it and even in her half-awake state, she knew she looked good.

Adam paused less than a foot away and lifted a hand to tip her chin up with one long tanned finger. The expression in his eyes was hooded and impossible to read. Heat, most definitely, and maybe a little amusement but she thought she caught the same sharp yearning that lanced through her.

"Good morning, Samantha," he murmured before dropping a kiss on her startled mouth. The first kiss was featherlight. The next lingered. The third turned into more than a hello. A *lot* more.

Her reserve melted away and she gave a soft mewl that was a mix of surprise and longing. Before she knew it, she was plastered up against him, her mouth clinging enthusiastically to his. Once her ears were buzzing and her skin tingling, Adam drew back, his eyes dark and slumberous.

Sucking in air, she then let it escape in a shuddery gush before realizing that her hands had fisted his shirt as though she were afraid he'd vanish. It took a concerted effort to unclench her fingers one at a time and smooth the wrinkled fabric with hands that shook.

All she could manage was a hoarse, "*Wow.*"

"Yeah." His voice was deep and raspy, his

breathing almost as ragged as hers. "That was some hello but maybe we should leave before it turns into something else."

"Something—?" She blinked his face into focus. "Oh…um—right." Color high, she stepped back on wobbly legs and nervously slid her tongue along her bottom lip. "That might—um, be for the b-best." Spinning away to reach for her shoulder bag with hands that trembled, Sam rolled her eyes because even to her own ears she'd sounded disappointed. Disappointed that he hadn't ravished her like the last time.

Her breath escaped in an audible whoosh. *Oh, boy.*

Adam chuckled and when she straightened, dropped a friendly kiss on her neck. He slid his palm down her back to the base of her spine and even though she knew it was just to guide her out the door, she shivered because she had a feeling all her good intentions—her careful planning— were about to go up in smoke.

And she couldn't have cared less.

Studying him out of the corner of her eye, Sam couldn't help noticing that he drove as he did everything else, with casual competence and complete mastery. She'd told herself that sneaking into the surgical observation rooms to watch him had simply been professional curiosity when the truth was she hadn't been able to stay away.

Before she could stop it, a tingle began at the bottom of her spine and worked its way up to the base of her skull because she knew from experience that he did other things just as masterfully. Things she'd told herself her memory had exaggerated. Things that would be easy to forget. That *he* would be easy to forget.

Fat chance. Especially after that kiss.

She'd told him she needed space and then ignored her own protestations because she'd had an almost overwhelming need to see him. She was rabidly curious about a man who could look at her with hot intensity one minute and then deliver a baby the next; a man who'd said he wasn't about to ignore what had happened in San Francisco and then promptly did.

Huddling against the door to put as much distance between them as she could, Sam realized that he was dressed pretty much as she remembered him in San Francisco—faded jeans worn almost white in places and a black T-shirt that emphasized his warm coppery skin.

It had something very un-Sam-like stirring beneath her skin. Like "Amanda" was restless to emerge. Like her alter ego was lifting her head, sucking in air as she closed her eyes to concentrate on identifying the deliciously heady scent of him—warm and spicy with a subtle hint of bergamot.

A little freaked by the realization that she was starting to sound crazy even in her own head, she sneaked another peek at him and found him studying her with eyes as warm and spicy as he smelled. Her pulse gave a funny little lurch, and for an instant, her belly went airborne.

"So. Where are we going again?" she asked a little desperately.

"Juniper Falls."

"It sounds rustic."

Adam's grin was quick and white in the pre-dawn darkness as he took the interstate on-ramp and accelerated south. "You sound worried."

She nibbled on her lip and nervously smoothed her skirt over her thighs. "Should I be? Worried, I mean?"

She felt his eyes on her profile. "Are you?" His voice reached across the Jeep's darkened cab, a rough and tempting challenge that scraped at the sensual nerve endings she hadn't thought she had.

"Well," she rasped, a little light-headed. "Only if you're kidnapping me."

His soft chuckle soothed the little pulse bump. "As tempting as that sounds, that isn't the reason for our field trip."

"Oh?" Heck, had that sounded as disappointed as she felt?

Instead of replying, he checked his side mirrors before accelerating around a truck. Once they were some distance away, he said casually, "Coco thought you might like to see where the foundation started."

Perturbed by the disappointment that it had been Coco's idea, all she could say was, "Why Juniper Falls?"

"I grew up there," he announced, and her disappointment morphed into curiosity. "Since it relies mostly on tourists all year round there isn't—wasn't—a proper hospital, which meant no medical care, especially for the folks who can't afford to travel to larger centers. I started the outreach program for people who can't afford specialist care."

She sat up slowly and studied him curiously. "*You* started the foundation?"

He grimaced. "Unofficially. It was just an idea until I took the concept to Coco," he corrected. "She has all the contacts. So we set things up and now it's not just about Juniper Falls anymore. There are dozens of people who donate their time and skills to the foundation in other small towns."

"Maybe," she conceded. "But *they* don't have a foundation named after them, do they?"

He made a sound of exasperation in the back of his throat. "How on earth did you reach that conclusion?"

"Oh, come on," she snorted, turning to grin at him. "Surely, I'm not the only one to make a connection between Galahad and Knight?"

He met her gaze for just a moment and she lost herself in the warm amber depths of his eyes.

"You know," he said, when her amusement faded beneath his intense scrutiny, "that's the first time I've heard you laugh. Really laugh, I mean."

"That's ridiculous," she scoffed, smoothing her hair off her forehead in a move she recognized as nervousness. "I laugh all the time."

He shook his head. "Not with me." His gaze caressed her face, coming to land on her mouth before returning to the road. He was smiling when he said, "I like it."

A shocked little bubble grew in her chest. Something that felt very much like pleasure. Horrified by how much his words affected her; how much she'd needed that brief acknowledgment of an attraction that went beyond the physical, she rasped, "You're changing the subject, Dr. Knight."

He chuckled, the deep warmth of it reminding her that she might have said he'd been her rebound rebellion but she hadn't been able to forget how he'd made her feel and she hadn't been able to stay away despite her determination to treat him as nothing more than an occasional boss or colleague.

To distract herself from the direction her thoughts were heading, she finally asked, "Are you going to tell me what prompted you to start the foundation?"

He flicked a hooded look in her direction before returning his gaze to the road. After a long pause, he said, "My grandmother died of a heart condition that shouldn't have killed her." He was silent for some time before adding, "My father was an artist, more concerned with the contents of a bottle than with making a living—at least after I was born. Needless to say, there wasn't a lot of money and she kept quiet about her condition until it was too late."

She heard what he didn't say. "And your mother?"

His mouth twisted an instant before he gave a short hard laugh. "She wasn't around."

"Oh?" she said carefully, wondering if his mother had died. "I'm sorry."

"Don't be," he drawled dryly. "She wasn't."

"Oh?" she said again, her brow tightening at his tone more than his words. "Why do you say that?"

After a short pause, he admitted, "The instant

I was born, she handed me over to my father and told us to have a nice life."

Sam couldn't hide her shock. "He—he *told* you that?"

"Every time he got drunk," Adam said casually, as though he were talking about some acquaintance. "He'd lock himself in his studio and stare at the paintings he'd done of her. And then he'd cry and quietly put away the contents of an entire bottle of whatever he had in the house."

Sam swallowed past the lump in her throat at the image he'd painted of a man devastated by the loss of someone he'd loved. "He must have loved her very much."

She wasn't sure what to make of his dry snort.

"He was obsessed with a woman he couldn't have," he said dispassionately as though he were talking about a stranger. "Her parents wanted a commemoration of her coming of age. Apparently, it's a thing among socialites of wealthy families, but then I suppose you'd know more about that than I would." He sent her an unreadable glance, but before she could say that she hadn't run with that crowd, he continued, "Anyway, they heard about this up-and-coming Native American artist and decided to one-up their friends. Of course, he didn't do portraits and initially refused the offer, that is until he got a look at his subject. She was everything he wasn't—

a blue-eyed blonde that simply drew everyone in with her bright and bubbly blue-blooded gorgeousness." This time Sam had no trouble interpreting his snort.

"Well, long story short, he fell like a rock and thought she'd fallen too. When she announced that she was pregnant, he was over the moon because now her family would surely allow them to be together." He gave a hard laugh. "Yeah, well, the laugh was on him because it turns out she was already engaged to some rich blue-blooded guy and had no intention of giving up her bright and golden future for a struggling artist from the reservation. She'd only been having her last fling before tying the knot. A baby with him didn't exactly feature in her plans other than to punish her parents."

Sam's mind whirled as she considered his words. "She—she was a debutante?"

"Coincidence, huh?"

Sam didn't know what he meant, but before she could ask, he whipped into a small local strip mall. He parked and with a terse, "Wait here," slid out of the car and disappeared into the bakery, leaving Sam with her thoughts whirling.

Minutes later, he was back, handing over a large to-go mug and a small bakery box. Conscious that he'd used the stop to close the subject, she took the coffee and peeked into the box at the assorted pastries. They smelled fresh, warm and very tempting, but in that instant she couldn't have swallowed one mouthful if her life depended on it.

"You eat pastries for breakfast?"

He backed out of the parking spot and headed for the exit. "They're for you."

"I don't normally eat breakfast," she said absently, as he turned onto the road heading east again, studying him out the corner of her eye.

She caught sight of his wry half smile before he said, "Maybe that's why you're so cranky in the morning."

"I am not cranky," she said primly, unsure whether to be relieved or disappointed by the subject change but willing to give him space. Heck, she understood all too well the baggage that came with family. "I'm just not a morning person." His answer was a low chuckle that eased her clenched gut. Apparently, talking about his family made him as cranky as he accused her of being. "At least not when I'm rudely awakened before the birds."

He flashed her a sizzling look, his mouth curving with sensuality. "I could help with that," he drawled, the deeply sensual timbre of his voice sliding into her belly like a heated promise because there was absolutely no doubt about what he meant.

She snorted and inhaled sharply at the exact moment she took a sip of coffee and everything went down the wrong way. She instantly went into a paroxysm of coughing. Preoccupied with hacking up a lung, she felt the car pull over and the to-go cup whipped out of her hand, the next instant receiving a couple of hard whacks to her back. It finally did the job, and after a few more splutters, she managed to drag in a shuddery breath as she held up a hand of surrender and collapsed back into her seat.

A large hand gently cupped her chin and tipped her face sideways. "You okay?" he murmured, his eyes quickly assessing her in a way that was both professional and intensely personal, leaving her feeling exposed.

"Define okay?" she rasped, brushing his hand away before she decided she liked it there. She sat up and reached for her shoulder bag to look for a tissue.

Adam snagged it from her nerveless fingers and again tilted her face toward him. She was surprised enough by his move that she let him gently and efficiently dab at her face and wet eyes. His mouth quirked as he caught her gaze.

"Interesting that the idea of my helping to improve your morning mood makes you choke," he said, studying her intently in the light from the dash. "Why is that, I wonder?"

Her face heated. "You had your chance and blew it," she dismissed loftily, snatching the tissue from his hand and stuffing it back in her purse. Then because she was tempted to crawl into his lap and bury her face in his throat, she shifted back, hoping to put a little distance between them. "I was just a little stunned by your arrogance, that's all. Besides—" she waved her hand flippantly as he pulled back onto the road "—many have tried and failed."

Now why had she said that, she wondered when one dark brow rose up his forehead and his eyes turned almost black. She shivered. Heck, he must know from her behavior that she wasn't nearly as sophisticated as her words implied. Or, at least, *suspect* that she wasn't.

"Many huh?" he drawled—and there was that bite of annoyance again—studying her in the light from the dash. "Does that include last night's date?"

Sam frowned, confused. "Last night's—? What are you talking about?"

"Coco said you were out to dinner last night." He paused, his eyes unreadable, mouth unsmiling.

"Oh," she said, thinking back to the subtle bite of displeasure in his voice when he'd arrived at her door. As though he were jealous of her *date*, which had actually been a business dinner and had not exactly gone well. Blake Lowry had kind of hinted that any sizeable donation he made came with strings. The kind that led to the bedroom. Needless to say, she'd cut the evening short.

"Blake is a wonderful man." No, he wasn't. But she wasn't about to tell Adam that. Anyway, let him think what he wanted. Sam didn't have anything to hide.

"Blake?" He grimaced as though the name pained him. "So he's what, some male model or something?"

Sam snorted out a laugh. "Don't be snide," she chastised mildly. "He's actually a financial director at the tech company his father owns."

"Uh-huh," he said finally, sending her a hooded glance as he flipped his indicator and turned onto a gravel road, the Jeep's headlights slicing through the darkness. "And does this financial director fit into that ridiculous plan of yours?"

Alerted to something in his voice, Sam paused in selecting a cinnamon-covered doughnut hole from the bakery box and slid him a curious look. "Actually, no," she snapped. "For your information, my plan is *not* ridiculous." He didn't comment but the glance he sent her spoke volumes about his opinion. "It makes perfect sense when you're changing your life."

"Uh-huh. So Jake's—what?"

"A potential donor," she snapped, shoving the doughnut hole into her mouth. "And it's Blake."

"Ah. So it was a business dinner."

She looked up and narrowed her eyes when she caught the amused curve of his mouth, as though the news pleased him. Annoyed with that smug look, she opened her mouth to deny it out of irritation but was distracted when the headlights picked out an arched-stone-and-iron gateway over which the words *Copper Creek Aviation* were displayed.

Her mouth closed with a snap and an uncomfortable feeling settled in her belly. It might have been the result of the three doughnut holes she'd just wolfed down, but was more likely the uneasy feeling that they were about to board an aircraft that in no way resembled anything she'd ever flown in.

"Please tell me that we're about to board a large commercial jet with in-flight attendants."

He laughed as though she'd made another joke, when she'd been serious as a heart attack. "Nope, Miss City Girl. Where we're going, there's no place for anything larger than a twin prop." Fried dough abruptly churned in her belly as he pulled up in front of a sprawling building. With the sky only just beginning to lighten, the place appeared deserted. "But not to worry," Adam assured her lightly, "I have a couple hours flying time, and last week I learned how to land without the instructor."

Sam felt her eyes widen and tightened her grip on the rapidly cooling coffee. "You mean— *you're* flying?"

He must have heard something in her voice because he turned to study her face in the darkened interior of the cab, his gaze abruptly serious. "Yes, I'm flying." After a short silence, during which she struggled to absorb the news, he asked quietly, "You trust me?"

Sam gave a strangled laugh. "If I needed heart surgery, maybe," she managed, exhaling on a gusty whoosh. "But this—this is something completely different. I, uh—"

"Hey," he interrupted gently, lifting a hand to cup her face and gently swipe his thumb along her tight jaw. The gesture was both an apology and intended to soothe. While it did just that, it also sparked a host of sensations that weren't the least soothing.

Dammit, she thought, struggling not to lean into his touch. She was in a bad way when just the touch of his hand on her face had the hard knot of fear melting. His deep voice slid across the space, settling alongside the feelings she was already fighting for this complex man. Feelings that were as thrilling as they were terrifying.

"I was kidding," he said softly. "I've logged over thirty-two-hundred hours in the air and I've been doing this since I was in high school."

"Doing what exactly?" Sam choked out. "Abducting women?"

He traced a finger along her collarbone. "Nope," he said with a grin when she shivered. "I've never had to do that before."

She could believe it. Just take her for example. Ever since she'd fallen into his lap in San Francisco, she'd been fighting the urge to follow him anywhere. She might say that she was annoyed to be dragged out before the sun was even up but the terrifying truth was that something deep inside had shuddered awake when she opened her door to find him on her doorstep looking better than coffee and doughnuts.

If *that* wasn't a sign she was in *big* trouble, then she hadn't been paying attention.

CHAPTER EIGHT

ADAM SLID HIS gaze to the woman white-knuck-
ling it beside him. She was pale and tense but had
uttered not one word since that strangled gurgle
back when she'd first caught sight of their ride.

"Hey," he said softly, infusing his voice with
confidence. "I know this isn't what you were
expecting, but this is a solid little plane and the
mechanic keeps her in tip-top condition."

With her fingers digging into the seat, Sam
looked around the tiny cockpit. "There's not a
lot of plane between me and the ground," she admitted into the headset. A visible shiver moved
through her. "And those propellers look kind of
flimsy. In fact, this whole aircraft looks flimsy."

"Relax," his deep voice soothed. "This girl
is the best twin turboprop on the market. She's
solid and reliable and can withstand anything but
major weather. Besides—" he said, gesturing to
the landscape below "—you don't see scenery
like this from a commercial jet."

Instead of agreeing, Sam ignored the view and kept her eyes locked on him. "Did you know that nearly four-hundred people die in private plane accidents every year?"

"That fatality rate is negligible compared to the thirty-thousand road accident deaths," he pointed out, hoping facts would ease the hollow-eyed fear. "That works out to be about one per one-hundred-thousand flying hours, which is nothing. You have a better chance of dying walking across a street than you do in an aircraft." Unable to keep his hands to himself, he took one hand off the controls and smoothed the wrinkle between her brows, enjoying the softness of her skin. "We'll be fine, Miss Worrywart. Just sit back and enjoy the new experience."

For reasons he couldn't think about now, he wanted to share his love of flying with her.

Grabbing his hand, she returned it to the controls. "Hands back on those controls, buster," she squawked, making him chuckle and link their hands. He enjoyed her surprise and the perceptible tremble in the pale elegant fingers and the way her eyes darkened and her breath caught as her fingers clenched in his.

Looking down at their entwined hands, he marveled at how different they were, at how good her hand looked and felt in his—his large and dark, hers pale and slender. It was as if they'd been molded to fit together like pieces of a puzzle.

He gave her hand a last squeeze before releasing it, because not only was that kind of thinking sappy and *way* out of his comfort zone—probably because it reminded him of his father—he felt like he was free-falling through space without a parachute.

It would be wise to remember that wanting something didn't always make it happen.

Just ask his old man.

Ninety minutes later, Adam pulled into the tree-shaded parking area of a two-story building tucked against the side of the mountain, overlooking the narrow valley below.

"What is this place?" Sam asked curiously, taking in the surroundings, the neat gardens and sprawling green lawns.

"Juniper Falls Medical Center. It's pretty basic but handles all local medical and emergency care. Anything they can't cope with gets flown to the closest large center."

It looked more like a ski lodge than a hospital. "A hospital?" she asked, studying the building and wondering why she got the feeling he was waiting for her reaction. "Why does it look like a ski lodge?"

Adam laughed, and for the first time seemed

relaxed. "That's because it is. Or was. With the town growing to accommodate the increase in tourists, the lodge owners needed more space, so they sold and moved farther out of town. Since the building was already here, it made sense to renovate instead of starting from scratch."

Sam was quiet as she studied the view of the town nestled in the valley. It was a gorgeous, tranquil setting that tugged at a memory buried deep inside her.

"Do you remember when I told you I used to think I'd been abducted by aliens as a child?" She saw his lips curve into a smile and laughed at the memory. "Well, I used to fantasize they'd taken me from a place like this."

Pulling his keys from the ignition, he turned toward her and Sam felt the brush of his gaze. It made her feel vulnerable and exposed so instead of meeting his eyes, she kept her face averted.

After a moment's silence he said, "You didn't like growing up rich?"

Sam nibbled on her lip because she sensed that to dismiss her affluent childhood would be to denigrate his. "I think—I think I would have preferred a mom who baked cookies and tucked me in at night," she admitted quietly. "A mom who wasn't always too busy to attend my ballet recitals."

"Yeah," he said quietly after a short silence.

"Me too." She turned and caught his quick mouth quirk as he shook his head. With a soft laugh, he opened the door and got out. Before closing it, he looked at her. "But I'd have skipped the ballet recitals too."

Only mildly offended because she had a feeling he was deliberately trying to lighten the mood, Sam scrambled after him. "You're such a *guy*," she accused, clamping down on the inexplicable emotion grabbing her by the throat when his deep chuckle resonated deep inside her. Emotion she had no business feeling for a man she'd insisted on labeling a rebound rebellion.

Inhaling the fresh mountain air, she let her gaze drift to the shifting muscles in his back, down to a really world-class ass cupped in soft worn denim and felt her chest ease. Physical attraction, it seemed, was easier to handle—and ignore—than emotions.

"So," she said lightly, "what *did* you do as a kid?"

He turned and nearly caught her ogling his body. Cheeks warming, Sam met his gaze with big innocent eyes. With a knowing look, he handed over a bulging briefcase. "Hold that, will you." She took it, pretending the brush of his fingers didn't send tingles shooting up her arm.

He looked toward the mountains, then

scratched his jaw and shrugged as his gaze returned to hers. "What every kid out here does, I guess."

"And that is?"

"My cousins and I ran wild. Fishing, hiking, skiing, riding, camping and—" he chuckled "—chasing girls, of course."

She grunted softly at the image of a young Adam chasing girls and dismissed the little shaft of jealousy that lodged right beside her heart.

"Of course you did," she muttered dryly, imagining him at seventeen sending young girls aflutter with a heavily lashed amber-eyed look. Heck, she wasn't even an impressionable adolescent and he made *her* flutter.

She imagined the little boy whose mother had waltzed off to her fairy-tale life, uncaring how much her actions had hurt her lover and the infant she'd blithely given up. She couldn't conceive of abandoning a child she'd carried—and come to love—for nine months, even if she didn't want to be with the father.

For a moment, she let herself imagine what would have happened if her weekend in San Francisco had resulted in a child. A warm little glow sparked in the center of her chest even as her belly dipped at the image of a dark-haired, dusky-skinned baby staring up at her with serious amber eyes.

God, she thought as her heart clenched with yearning. *How could anyone walk away from that?*

It was on the tip of her tongue to ask if he'd ever met his mother but he'd already turned away to reach for a large box and the moment was lost. Finally, with a hooded look in her direction, he shut the door and took off toward the portico entrance of Juniper Falls Medical Center.

Lifting her face to the crisp mountain air and warm sun, Sam paused a moment before following more slowly. She was bewildered by the emotions swirling inside her and needed a moment to steady herself. Despite her growing unwanted feelings for a man who was way out of her league, she felt happy—perhaps for the first time in way too long—which was reason enough to be cautious.

He stirred up emotions she didn't have a clue how to handle or interpret and wasn't sure she liked.

Seriously though. She'd recently broken off a relationship with a man she'd thought she'd spend the rest of her life with, so how was it that she was feeling things for another man that she'd never felt for Lawrence?

No sooner had they crossed the parking area

than the front doors flew open and a slight figure emerged at a run to fling herself at Adam. Since he was carrying a box of medical supplies, he caught her one-handed before she knocked them both to the ground.

"Adam." The girl laughed and hugged him tightly. "We've been waiting for ages. What took you so long?"

"Since it's barely seven, it can't have been that long," he chuckled, dropping a kiss on her forehead and turning to introduce Sam who'd been standing there, feeling a little stunned. "This is Samantha Jefferies," he said to the girl. "She's the angel who's taken over running the foundation. I wanted to introduce her to everyone and show her where it all started."

Studying the way Adam tucked the young woman against his side, Sam wondered at the sharp pain in her chest. He'd introduced her as nothing more than a colleague. Which was fine, she told herself as she unclenched her fingers from the briefcase to transfer it to her other hand. It was exactly what she wanted. Wasn't it?

"Hello."

"Hi, I'm Leah," the young woman said, stepping away from Adam to grab Sam's hand between hers and Sam couldn't help but notice how beautiful and delicate she was, with long glossy dark hair, dusky skin and large almond eyes. The sight of her beside Adam, slender and graceful as a deer, made Sam feel like a clumsy Amazon in comparison.

Before she could reply, Adam checked his watch. "Leah's a med student at Stanford," he said briskly. "She's been working summers here in one capacity or another since high school. No one knows this place better, so I've asked her to give you the VIP tour since I have a full day ahead. Don't let her talk your ear off." With that, he shifted the box and leaned toward her.

For an instant, she thought he might kiss her but he simply relieved her of the briefcase and turned away, leaving Sam staring after him in bewilderment, a hollowness blooming in her chest because he suddenly seemed like a stranger.

Because there was something between him and Leah?

Feeling hurt and ridiculously like she'd been abandoned, Sam schooled her features and turned to find Leah frowning at Adam's disappearing back.

"What's up with *him*?" the younger woman muttered before turning speculative eyes Sam's way. She shrugged, as baffled by his odd behavior as she was embarrassed by her own. She'd almost—*almost*—leaned into him for that "kiss" and cringed inwardly at the thought of how he would have handled it if she had.

Oh, God. She really needed to get a grip.

There was an awkward moment as Sam tried to ignore the other woman's curiosity before finally exhaling in a long gush. "Look," she said, turning to look the girl in the eye. "I'm really sorry to be dumped on you like this. You're obviously busy so maybe I should just head back to town. I'm sure I could keep myself busy until Adam is ready to leave." Either that or she could hire a car and return to San José.

"No way." Leah's response was immediate and fierce. "That'll be hours. Besides," she said, studying Sam openly with her large almond-shaped eyes, "I've been dying to meet you."

Surprised, Sam blinked at the young woman and wondered if she'd heard correctly. "You... have?"

"Uh-huh." She laughed when she caught Sam's expression. "Oh, not from Adam," she snorted cheerfully. "He *never* talks about his private life. I heard all about you from Dr. Rutherford."

Sam's eyebrows shot into her hairline. After a couple of beats, she gave a tight laugh, wondering what Aunt Coco had said and why she hadn't prepared Sam for this girl, this town—well, this field trip. "Oh. Well, don't feel bad." To give herself a moment, she lifted a hand to tuck an escaped lock of hair behind her ear. "He's told me nothing about you either." She gestured to the hospital and the town. "Or any of this."

Leah's dark eyes twinkled. "That's okay." She grinned. "I'm sure you have other things to talk about."

"Wh-what?" Sam blinked as her mouth dropped open. "Oh, no," she said hastily, wondering at the relationship between Adam and this gorgeous creature. "It's not what you think. We work together. Sort of." She sighed. "It's complicated."

"Isn't love always?"

"Love?" Sam said aghast. "Oh, no. No," she said again when Leah cocked her head, long silky dark strands brushing a slender shoulder. "We've just kind of met," she explained, ignoring the heat rising in her cheeks at the girl's expression. She ended with a lame, "Besides, we work together."

Leah snorted. "I've known Adam a long time and I've never seen him look at anyone the way he looked at you just now." She gave a dramatic shiver that made Sam roll her eyes.

"Like he couldn't wait to get away?"

Leah's brow wrinkled and her eyes narrowed on Sam's face. "No," she said slowly, contemplatively. "It wasn't like that at all."

Not wanting to think about what it was, Sam

used the moment to shove the hair off her forehead. "Why are you doing this?"

"Adam asked me to."

Sam's eyes widened in surprise. Okay, so
maybe it was closer to shock, but what the heck?
"Adam asked you to interfere in his personal
life?"

For a couple of beats, Leah stared at her un-
comprehendingly, then she burst out laughing.
"Heck no," she giggled finally. "He'd skin me
alive if he knew."

"Then why, when you're clearly in love with
him yourself?"

"*What?* No." She gave an amused snort and
caught Sam's hand in hers. "I love Adam, sure,"
she said tugging her in the direction Adam had
gone. "But like an honorary uncle or something.
I'm only twenty-two so he's way too old."

"He's not that old," Sam defended him hotly.

Leah grinned knowingly and steered Sam
across the lobby. "Much older brother then," she
said cheekily. "But it's interesting how quickly
you defended him."

It was mid-morning when Adam decided to take
a detour to the wards before hunting down some
food. Most of the patients he treated here had little or no health insurance and many came from
the tribal lands nearby. They were people who

would probably die without the procedures and hospital care the foundation covered. And because today was mainly follow-ups, part of his mind had been occupied elsewhere.

In truth, he'd kept seeing Samantha's face. Firstly, when he'd deliberately pulled Leah close, hoping the move would put a little distance between them—especially after the stuff he'd revealed about his past—and then as he'd reached for his briefcase. For just a moment, she'd stilled as though he'd been about to kiss her. He'd seen it in her widening eyes and the hitch in her breath. And damn if he hadn't been tempted. So tempted that he'd had to leave before he'd shocked both her *and* Leah.

He'd caught her embarrassed mortification as he'd spun away and had almost turned back. But he didn't want an audience for what he wanted to do with Samantha Jefferies. He was done giving her space and he was done pretending they didn't know each other.

The nurses' station was deserted. Hospitals tended to empty out ahead of the weekend, leaving only those too sick to be sent home. And since Juniper Falls wasn't a bustling metropolis, weekends at the medical center tended to be quiet.

So quiet that over the muted beep of equipment, he heard the low murmur of voices and then the unmistakable sound of throaty laughter that dug claws of lust and awareness into his gut.

Damn. He was in a bad way if just the sound of her voice had his skin itching and tightening. He'd tasted her again and wanted more. He wanted to wrap himself in her sweetness and was pretty sure after this morning that she did too.

"When I'm finished with you, Mrs. Jackson," he heard her say. "You'll be the belle of the ball."

"Call me Ida, dear," he heard, as he headed around the counter to access the computer. "Can I let you in on a little secret?"

"What's that?"

"In my day, I had a dozen beau all competing for my attention."

"I can believe it. You look gorgeous," Samantha declared with a chuckle. "Bart won't know what hit him."

"Oh, pooh." The woman snorted. "Bart Schmart. I was thinking more along the lines of that hunky Dr. Knight. He was here earlier and *hoo-wee*, that boy is hot tamales." Sam's warm laughter drifted seductively down the passage and Adam felt the back of his neck heat that he was eavesdropping on a discussion about himself.

"What do you think, Gladys?" the voice continued. "Should we introduce Samantha to our new beau and risk him falling for her?"

He was thinking that it was way too late for

that when an odd sound sent a shaft of foreboding spearing through him.

"Gladys, are you all right?" Mrs. Jackson demanded, then a more peremptory, *"Gladys!"*

He was rounding the counter when he heard, "Samantha, get the nurse and tell them to page the doctor. Hurry!" Her voice was strident but Adam caught the fear in the woman's voice. "Gladys, hang in there, you hear me. Don't you dare die on us. *Nurse!* Oh, Lord—"

Adam broke into a run, nearly colliding with Samantha on her way out of the ward. He instantly spun around, his hands closing instinctively around her arms to steady her before his forward momentum sent them both sprawling.

"Adam!" she gasped, her eyes huge and startlingly blue in her white face. "Oh, th-thank God. It's Mrs. Roscoe, she's—"

"Having a heart attack. Where is everyone? Where is Leah?" he demanded, pushing her firmly aside to stride into the room. He took in the situation at a glance. "Mrs. Jackson, you need to step aside."

"She was fine," the woman insisted, blinking rapidly as she scuttled out of the way. "Gladys was fine and all of a sudden she clutched her chest and made this awful sound. You're a doctor," she insisted, her voice wobbling alarmingly. "She isn't breathing. *Fix* her."

The woman on the bed was in her late seventies and clearly in distress. She was gasping and clawing at her chest, her throat. Adam snatched the oxygen mask from the wall and covered her nose and mouth, turning up the flow to full throttle. "Samantha," he rapped out, turning to see her hovering uncertainly in the doorway. "I need you to hold this."

"What—what about the n-nurse?" she croaked, looking a little wild-eyed as she hurried over to the bed.

"No time," he growled when Gladys abruptly went limp. "Hold this."

A slender hand instantly reached out, fingers visibly trembling and icy cold when they briefly covered his. He slid his hand free and began CPR, his gaze holding Samantha's. "Mrs. Jackson," he said calmly. "Could you please press the button on the wall above your bed?"

The other woman quickly reached over and activated the alarm. "I'll do one better," she told him briskly. "I'll find you a nurse."

"Tell them it's a code blue," he called out, as she hurried from the room. And with the sound of her slippers slapping smartly against the linoleum, Adam looked back to find Samantha's attention now locked on the still face in the bed. Her lips were pressed into a distressed line.

"Sam, honey," he said calmly and waited until

she looked up. His heart clenched at the sight of overly bright glassy eyes and the waxy complexion. "I know this is scary but I need you to listen carefully, okay?"

She sucked in a shaky breath and gave a jerky nod.

"Good girl. I can't stop chest compressions, so I want you to slip the face-mask elastic around the back of Gladys' head and tighten it." He waited patiently while she followed instructions, gently lifting the unconscious woman's head to fit the elastic band around the back of her head. "Now adjust it at the side where it joins with the mask. That's great," he encouraged when she tugged on the elastic until the mask fitted snugly to Gladys' face. "Okay, I want you to go to the nurses' station and find the crash cart and bring it here." She paused for an instant, her eyes sweeping up to meet with his. "It looks like a trolley with a lot of drawers."

She gave another jerky nod and hurried away, leaving Adam worried about her ragged breathing and the expression in her eyes. She was teetering on the edge of a panic attack and there was little he could do except try to talk her out of it while he worked to keep Gladys' heart pumping.

He paused to check the woman's carotid pulse, his mouth tightening when he found it weak and fluttery. She needed meds, he thought, as well as an emergency transfer to the nearest center equipped with a cardio-surgical unit or she wasn't going to make it.

The best he could do for Gladys now was to administer a series of drug cocktails to stabilize her heart and dissolve clots. The hospital didn't have a catheterization lab, an MRI or a surgical suite equipped to perform complicated heart surgery. All they could do, he thought as the sound of the trolley drew closer, was do a sonar and EKG before flying her out because most of the hospital's lab work was flown to Fresno.

He turned as Samantha rushed into the room, pushing the trolley ahead of her. "That's great," he said as she pulled the trolley up to the bed. "Now open the third tray and remove the bag that says dextrose and a five-ml syringe package."

CHAPTER NINE

EVERYTHING AROUND SAM FADED. Her muscles quivered with the need for flight but she forced her world to narrow to just her hands and the calm voice filling her head. Hands shaking uncontrollably, she followed Adam's instructions, fighting not to be sucked back into a past she thought she'd overcome.

Breath lodged in her throat, she was abruptly ten again and home alone with the housekeeper for company. As if she were experiencing the events of that long ago night, she heard again the loud thump over her thundering heartbeat; the sharp cry of someone in distress and then freezing with terror because there'd recently been a spate of home invasions...of finally creeping down the stairs to find Mrs. Hopkins collapsed on the kitchen floor...dialing 911...the house filling with police and paramedics—

"Samantha. *Sam!*" A sharp voice came to her from a distance. Barely aware that she was gasping for breath, she felt herself jostled aside as hands suddenly took over.

"We'll take it from here, hon."

Sam blinked and looked around, shocked to see people filling the room. When had they arrived? She'd heard nothing over the panicked rush of blood in her head as she'd automatically followed Adam's instructions.

Blinking away the black spots invading her vision, she backed away jerkily as several nurses blocked her view, the flurry of activity making her feel useless and inept. A fragile hand crept into hers and Sam dragged her eyes off the drama to see Ida Jackson looking as shaken as Sam felt.

"Let's g-go find some t-tea," she rasped, squeezing the old woman's hand and nudging her toward the door.

"Do you think we could add a d-dash of b-brandy to that?" Ida wobbled, her hand trembling uncontrollably. "Or maybe two?"

Fighting the chaotic emotions battling for control, Sam gave a ragged laugh that sounded a little too close to hysteria for comfort. She squeezed Ida's hand again and sent one last look over her shoulder at the tableau surrounding the bed where Adam, in the midst of the chaos, looked calm, skilled, in control and very much in his element.

At that moment, he looked up and their eyes met across the distance. Sam's breath caught in her throat. Everything in her stilled at the fierce emotions burning in Adam's amber gaze. His passion for his job. His grim determination to save the woman and the flash of awareness that it might not be enough.

With her heart clenching hard in her chest, she mouthed *I'm sorry* before hurrying from the ward, desperate to escape the feelings of inadequacy and shame that came in the wake of a panic attack.

Dammit, she'd thought she was getting over herself; thought she was overcoming the debilitating childhood affliction. Despair washed over her because she'd once again let everyone down because the insecure little kid inside her was terrified of failing. Terrified of losing someone else she cared about.

Oh, God. What must Adam think of her? That she couldn't even keep it together long enough to forget her insecurities and help save a dying woman.

Ten hours later, Adam drew the Jeep to a sliding stop before his cabin. The earlier hail had turned to snow, which was gusting around his Jeep, dropping visibility to a few feet. The weather forecast's predicted turbulent conditions had brought typical wild Sierra weather, and even if he hadn't flown to Fresno with medevac, the winds would have grounded his plane.

On their return, the pilot had been forced to make a detour when a group of hikers became stranded. It was now almost nine o'clock and he should have been exhausted. Yet, there was a low humming beneath his skin at the thought of Samantha waiting for him in his cabin.

Right. It somehow felt right.

Stilling, he studied the light spilling from the cabin windows and wondered if he'd somehow planned for this to happen. Although there hadn't been any question about accompanying Gladys to Fresno, he couldn't deny that he was glad the weather had grounded the plane.

He'd told Leah to book Samantha in at one of the numerous B&Bs but the girl had sent him a message that she'd dropped her off at his cabin. Instead of being elated at the thought of Samantha surrounded by his things, he should have been questioning Leah's motives.

His cabin was basic at best, not exactly the kind of place one took a blue-blooded princess.

Instantly, images of her earlier filled his mind. She'd bitten her lip, stiffened her spine and followed his instructions even as her fingers shook so badly she'd barely been able to hold the syringe. Yet, she'd held it together long enough for the nurses to arrive when he knew the panic attack had swooped over her like a dark cloud.

That last look over her shoulder had been filled with emotions that sliced right through him as she'd mouthed the words *I'm sorry*, and he wondered what had happened to put that look of shame and self-disgust in her eyes.

Adam reached for the bag of groceries, hoping she'd started a fire and helped herself to some of his clothes. It might be summer but up here in the Sierras, the weather could change in a matter of hours.

He shoved open the driver's door and was instantly assaulted by wind-driven ice and snow. Lurching from the Jeep, he slammed the door behind him and made a dash for the safety of the front porch. The little pellets of stinging ice were giving way to flakes that melted the instant they settled. *That could change*, he thought, shaking himself off before quietly slipping inside and shutting out the storm.

Once inside, Adam slid the bolt home and wiped moisture off his face. The faint glow coming from the fireplace did little to dispel the cold. Setting the groceries aside, he realized that Samantha hadn't added enough logs to heat the room.

He grimaced, reaching back to pull at the damp material clinging coldly to his skin. She had to be freezing, he thought, as he stripped off his shirt and used it to dry his face. Hell, *he* was freezing.

"Samantha?" he called softly, not wanting to startle her. "Sam?"

The only sound in the cabin was the shifting of logs in the fireplace and the lazy crackle of wood. For one horrible instant he thought that the cabin was empty, that she'd become tired of waiting and left. His gut instantly tightened. Maybe she'd thought she could walk into town and became disoriented. Maybe she'd wandered off the road and tumbled down the mountain or maybe—

He stopped when he realized what he was doing. Hell, he was losing it. Losing it over a woman who pulled him closer with one hand while pushing him away with the other. A woman, who despite the trappings of her child-hood, was warm and sweet. A woman who was vulnerable but not stupid.

Of course, she wouldn't leave. She was smart and resourceful—but she was a city girl completely out of her depth in the wilderness, and would hardly go wandering off alone in the dark.

He knew this, yet he couldn't stop the images flashing through his mind of her out in that, alone. Lost, cold and afraid. He would never forgive himself if anything happened to—

A soft sigh interrupted his self-directed anger, drawing him into the room like she was a magnet and he slivers of iron filings. His relief at finding her curled up beneath the afghan that was usually draped on the back of the sofa, nearly brought him to his knees. He had to rub his face a few times before he could look at her and not completely unravel. Because there she was, face flushed and peaceful beneath the wild tangle of hair that reflected the flickering light from the dying fire.

Something wild and sweet and alien moved through him then; something so powerful that he had to turn away before he scooped her up and crushed her against him. The intensity of the primitive impulse left him shaken and drove him to the fireplace where he began to build a fire that would drive away the chill.

He could do that, he thought, rattled by more than the emotions bombarding him. Alien emotions he had no idea how to handle.

Once the flames licked greedily at the tower of logs, he rose with every intention of heading to the kitchen to begin preparations for their dinner. But the moment he turned, his gaze was drawn inexorably toward the sleeping woman now half on her back, one arm flung above her head, the throw pooled at her waist.

His eyes traced her creamy features, the heavy

lacy crescents of her eyelashes resting against her flushed cheeks. The tousled mass of hair, tumbling across the cushion in wild disarray invited him to bury his face and hands in the fragrant cloud—and just breathe her in.

Her mouth, a full soft bow, parted on a quiet sigh as though she were dreaming. A heated spike of longing arrowed through him, and even as he instructed himself to move away, he was dropping to his haunches beside the couch.

God. She looked so lovely with firelight gilding her flawless skin and setting fire to the heavy spill of warm chestnut locks. His breath caught and he could not resist reaching out to trace the elegant arch of one eyebrow; smooth a silky lock of hair off her forehead with a cautious finger.

Almost imperceptibly, her breathing changed, her eyelashes fluttering as though she'd felt that whisper-soft touch in her sleep. She shifted languorously, her head rolling toward him. He was unable to resist touching her again—just the brush of his thumb across her cheekbone.

A low sound of yearning hummed in the back of her throat and more than anything, Adam wanted to cover her mouth with his and catch that husky sound for himself. He wanted to taste her need and let her taste his.

"Hey," he murmured, and her eyelashes fluttered again, then rose a fraction of an inch. The usually vibrant blue depths of her eyes were hazy and soft with sleep. He held his breath because watching her awaken was the most erotic thing he'd ever seen.

"Adam?" She breathed out a husky question that had something primal slamming into him like a one-two punch to the solar plexus; violent feelings he'd never felt for anyone let alone a woman from a world he despised. Feelings of need, lust, possessiveness and the overwhelming compulsion to protect.

Inhaling to clear his head, he drew the scent of her into his lungs instead. She smelled of soft warm woman with a hint of something fresh and clean. Like something he'd yearned for his entire life.

His throat tightened along with his gut. "Yeah," he said roughly. "Sorry I'm late. I tried to get here sooner but we had to rescue a couple of stranded hikers on the way back."

Awareness sharpened her gaze and she sat up abruptly, forcing him back a couple of inches. "*Ohmigod*," she burst out. "You flew in *that*? How's Gladys? When did you get back? Are the hikers okay? Are *you* okay?"

She shoved her hair off her face, eyes huge and distressed as they swept over him, presumably to check for injuries, before coming back to his. Completely against his will, Adam felt the pull of those endlessly blue depths and couldn't recall the last time any woman had expressed such genuine concern for him. Coco maybe, but then again she'd been more mother than mentor.

"Gladys is hanging on, the hikers will be okay and I'm good," he murmured. *Now.* Now that he was inches away from her and breathing in the scent of her skin, feeling the gentle heat pulsing off her body and the siren call that he'd tried but could no longer resist.

With his gaze locked on hers, he shifted closer, lifting his hand to gently trace the elegant line of her jaw and neck. He settled his thumb gently over the pulse beating a rapid tattoo in her throat, feeling it throb with life—and excitement.

It lit an answering call in his blood.

"You sound as though you were worried about me."

"I—of course, I was worried," she burst out indignantly. "I'd be worried about anyone caught in that."

Adam chuckled and brushed his thumb repeatedly against the delicate skin covering that fluttering pulse. She might deny there was anything between them but she couldn't control that little telltale response.

"Anyone?" he murmured deeply. "Are you sure you weren't just a little bit worried I might end up smashed against the side of the mountain?"

Her breath caught and she tried to jerk away in protest. "That's not funny, Adam," she rasped, wrapping long elegant fingers around his wrist. Her eyes flared with anger and something that instantly roused his blood. Instead of pushing him away, her gaze locked with his and, abruptly tired of hiding his feelings, he made no attempt to disguise the heat and emotions pumping through him.

Seconds ticked by as they breathed heavily into the heated silence until with a shuddery exhalation, her gaze dropped to his mouth with a sweep of heavy lashes. Beneath his thumb, her pulse stuttered, then sped up and she finally made a jerky, involuntary little move that brought her mouth closer to his. Then she stilled, tension humming in the air.

Her throat moved in a convulsive swallow that told him she wanted his mouth but was waiting for him to make the move and when he didn't, waiting for her to come to him, she made a hungry little sound in the back of her throat and jerked her gaze to his. The move had her parted lips brushing his, her eyes darkening until only a thin circle of cobalt surrounded large deeply black pupils. And because he was still touching her, he felt the helpless shudder move through her.

Whether she was deliberately drawing out the

tension, ratcheting up the need, Adam wasn't certain. He wasn't a green boy but a jolt moved through him at that barely-there touch. His skin buzzed with the growing compulsion to crush her mouth beneath his and take what they both wanted.

"Adam?" she murmured on a shuddery gust of yearning that had his awareness narrowing until the rest of the world faded. In that moment, the entire mountain range could have slid into the Yellowstone magma chamber and he wouldn't have noticed or cared.

"If you want it, Samantha," he growled hoarsely. "All you have to do is take it," he huffed out, when she blinked, looking drugged. Hell, he felt a little drugged himself. "You want it?" he taunted softly. "*You* take it."

"Just—take?" she breathed, sounding as though the idea had never occurred to her. And because he already knew that she wasn't nearly as self-assured and experienced as she appeared, Adam felt another crack appear in the wall he'd built around his heart.

This woman, he thought with surprised affection, for all her apparent sophistication and poise, was anything but. There was a vulnerability, a softness, that she couldn't quite hide from anyone paying attention. She felt too much and too deeply while pretending to be coolly reserved, and he suddenly understood that she'd shied away from medicine because she didn't know how to shield herself from the heartbreak that often accompanied the knowledge that not everyone could be saved.

She'd want to do that, he realized, recalling the way she sneaked into the children's ward to read to them, to give them a few moments of joy. Then he recalled how she'd given Gladys and Mrs. Jackson a makeover because being ill chipped away at one's self-esteem.

She'd want to save everyone and when she couldn't, it would devastate her.

A rush of emotion squeezed his chest in a vice-like grip. She was sweet and feisty and so desperate to hold herself aloof, hide her vulnerability. But he wanted her vulnerability and sweet warmth. He wanted her to give them to him.

Hell, he wanted her to give him everything.

Planting his hands on the sofa, on either side of her hips, he leaned closer and gathered the cool material of her dress in both hands.

"Take it," he taunted softly. "Take what you want." He waited a couple of beats before closing the distance between their mouths and then adding, "I…dare…you," so softly the words puffed against her lips.

She was so close that he could see each blue, silver and turquoise striation in her irises. Her eyelashes fluttered once before her chin dipped and with a shuddery breath, settled her lips lightly on his. After a couple of heartbeats, her gaze lifted and something warm and mischievous sparked in the darkened depths, bewitching him. Her lips parted on a quick grin and before he could anticipate her intention, she closed her teeth on his bottom lip and tugged gently.

The unexpectedness of that cheeky nip jolted him, sent fire racing across his skin. His hands clenched into fists to keep from yanking her closer. Locking his muscles, he hummed in the back of his throat.

Again, she surprised him. Closing her lips around his bottom lip, she sucked it into the moist warmth of her mouth before releasing it with a quiet pop. Then she began brushing her lips lightly along the length of his, flicking her tongue out in teasing swipes, making him wonder if she knew how close he was to losing control.

His skin buzzed, muscles tightened until he thought her next move would shatter his rapidly fraying control. Before long, he was growling low in his throat and sliding his tongue out to flick at the seam of her lips, tangle with her teasing tongue.

Unable to keep his hands to himself, he slid them beneath her skirt to smooth his palms up her thighs. Material bunching at his wrists, he headed north. Her breath hitched and she shivered, the long slender muscles quivering beneath silky skin. With a soft growl, she smoothed her palms up the slope of his arms, across the line of his shoulders to bury her fingers in his hair.

Then it was his turn to shudder, the sensation of her nails scraping his scalp, streaking the length of his spine, sending heat and lust clawing at his belly. He was rapidly spiraling out of control and he worried that when he did, he would be forever changed.

Unaware of the impending collapse of his iron control, Sam playfully evaded his teasing attempts to pursue her mouth, building the tension while he tamped down the primitive impulse to crush her close, to take what she was offering.

He knew the instant her teasing turned serious. Her fingers tightened and she murmured a command that finally snapped the fraying edges of his control. He opened his mouth and caught hers in a ravenous kiss the same moment his hands closed over her hips and tugged, rolling backward as she fell against him.

In an instant, he'd rolled her onto the thick rug before the fire, one thigh nudging hers apart as the kiss exploded. Wild and ravenous, then slow and deep, he took and gave back in equal measure until they were both breathless, writhing with need.

Frantic for the feel of smooth feminine skin sliding against his, for the hot intimate dampness of her need, Adam swept his hand up one long thigh until he encountered the narrow band of lace at her hips. Slipping his fingers beneath the elasticized lace, he tugged and quickly stripped the garment away, tossing the lace aside before cupping the soft firmness of her bottom in his hand.

He squeezed, and she moaned, arching into him as her nails trailed a torturous line of fire down his torso in retaliation. Her fingers curled into the waistband of his jeans, brushing his erection. He jolted at that teasing touch and, fearing he was seconds from embarrassing himself, he grabbed her hands.

"I've got this," he rasped in a voice he barely recognized as his own. *God*, he was so aroused that just the accidental brush of her finger across the wide sensitive crown had him shuddering like a kid.

Cursing the need to get naked, he yanked at the zipper and shoved his jeans and underwear down his legs. Even before the material cleared his ankles, she wrapped a hand around him and squeezed firmly enough to have his eyes roll back in his head.

"Not yet," he growled, gently removing her hand before he lost the last of his control and tore her dress in his desperation to get her naked. And he wanted her naked. He wanted to rediscover every inch of her lush body—every curve and dip and secret place. He wanted to taste the underside of her breast, curl his tongue around the tight pink bud and feast on her velvety skin. He *needed* to slide his mouth down her body, dip his tongue into her shallow belly button and then kiss her more intimately than any other man.

Adam's senses swam. Every touch felt new. Every hitched breath an aphrodisiac. He couldn't seem to decide what to sample next; what would elicit the most delicious shiver, the hungriest moan or the throatiest sigh.

San Francisco, it seemed, didn't count because he hadn't known her. Hadn't known the sound of her voice, the curve of her jaw and the way her eyes darkened when she was aroused. Now he could tell when she was nervous by the way she first licked and then nibbled on her bottom lip, the way warm color raced up her throat into her face.

Now he welcomed the hitch in her voice and the tiny shivers that moved across her skin. He wanted to fill his hands with her breasts and swallow the low sounds of her arousal because no woman had ever taken him from zero to a hundred in less time that it had taken for him to yank down his zipper.

"Adam—" she protested, and he quickly covered her mouth with his, snatching her breathless protest before it could fully form. He fed her kisses that were ravenous and just a little desperate, kisses that stripped him of his sanity and her of her protests.

She fisted his hair as their mouths tangled, giving him access to the rest of her body; access he ruthlessly exploited by bringing her to the edge over and over again until her breath was a ragged moan and her muscles quivered with the effort to reach for that elusive peak.

Glorying in her taste, the slide of her skin against his as she moaned and writhed, Adam mercilessly whipped the tension higher, tighter, until he was blind and deaf to anything but her pleasure. And when he joined their bodies with one hard thrust, she gave a sharp ragged cry, her body arching beneath his, her inner muscles clamping down on him like a hot fist.

He froze, panting roughly as she spasmed helplessly around him. "Did—?" he huffed tightly. "Are you okay?"

Sam opened her mouth but the only sound to emerge was a low breathless moan. She bit her lip and gave a quick jerky nod, her eyes blind and turned inward as her body undulated helplessly beneath his. "Don't stop," she gasped, wrapping her long legs around his hips and clutching at his shoulders as though she would bind him to her.

He wanted to tell her that there was nowhere he'd rather be but the sight of her beneath him, the feel of her around him fascinated him. It was nothing like he remembered. It was hotter... better...and in that moment she was the most beautiful thing he'd ever seen.

A flush of arousal stained her breasts, rushed across her chest and rose up her neck into her face. He wondered briefly how any man could look at her as she was now, head thrown back, lush curves and long slender limbs entwined with his, and want anyone else.

Slowly pressing deeper, Adam growled when she gasped and squirmed, yanking at his hair. "*Move!*" she ordered in a tight demanding voice, even as she arched her back and wrapped her limbs around him.

He simply tightened his grip and pressed her into the rug. "Look at me," he murmured deeply, and when her eyes fluttered open, the dazed expression in them nearly had him climaxing. "I want you to see *me* when you come."

"Adam—"

"Yeah," he growled roughly, leaning down to nip at her mouth. "*Me*. Only me."

And with his eyes locked on hers, he began to

move. Slowly at first with long measured strokes meant to gradually build the tension. But Sam wasn't interested in gradual and tried to force him to increase his pace when he wanted her blind to everything but him. He wanted her to see him, feel him, breathe him as he took her over.

And when her blue eyes went hazy and dark, those sexy little sounds that he'd never thought he'd hear again bursting erratically from her throat, he changed the tempo to shorter, harder strokes that jolted her and had her clenching even tighter around him.

He saw her eyes go wide the instant before her body bowed and shattered, the long low moan tearing from her throat.

The sight and sounds of her release triggered his own and he followed her over, pounding his way through his own climax until, with a grunt, he slammed home one last time and stilled, emptying himself into her shuddering body.

CHAPTER TEN

"So that's a yes?" Samantha asked calmly into the telephone while inside she was doing a little victory dance. She had one more donation for the foundation's first fundraising event with her at its helm. That it was a life-size sculpture—the centerpiece and drawcard she'd been looking for—meant it was guaranteed to generate a lot of interest. *And money.*

"That's very generous of you, Jack. I'll call you next week to arrange collection." She listened to his reply and then said, "Oh, no, it's the least we can do."

She thanked him again and disconnected, flushing at the memory of standing in his studio with her mouth hanging open after he'd asked if she'd consider modeling for him. It had been hugely embarrassing as the man was well-known for his erotic nudes.

Okay, so Jack Cesar was hot and fast becoming famous for his art, but there was no way she could get back to her plan with the memory of Juniper Falls so fresh in her mind. So she'd told him she was seeing someone, although she hadn't seen Adam since he'd dropped her off after that weekend.

From the moment she'd opened her eyes to find herself naked in an empty bed and the sounds of activity coming from the cabin's small kitchen, she'd started freaking out because their one-night stand had just become two. She could no longer tell herself that it had been the result of too much alcohol or the reaction of a woman discovering her fiancé with another man.

This time there was no rebellion to blame her actions on, only—oh, God, she was afraid to even think about *what* it was. She only knew that the previous twenty-four hours had irrevocably altered her opinion of Adam and wrecked the stability of her world.

When he'd dropped her off, she'd thanked him politely for the weekend, and belly cramping with nerves, told him nothing had changed when *everything* had changed.

For several heartbeats, he'd just looked at her and then the worst had happened. He calmly accepted her explanation, a hint of amusement in his eyes as he'd gently pushed her back against her front door, trapping her with his big body. Captured by his mesmerizing gaze, she hadn't put up even a token protest when his head had lowered and he'd caught her mouth in a kiss so potent it had scorched the bottom of her feet.

Just when she felt her body melt against his, he'd stepped back. With a, "See you soon," he'd casually descended the stairs, leaving her head buzzing with confusion.

Then she'd gotten mad, which had her even more confused because she had no right to be angry with him for giving her exactly what she'd said she wanted. It wasn't logical, it wasn't fair but she was learning firsthand that her feelings for him had no roots in logic.

Where they came from she wasn't sure—only that they were deep and terrifying.

Fortunately, she was busy planning her first charity event or she'd probably have gone insane obsessing about what he'd meant by that kiss and his parting remark. It was something she thought about constantly when she was alone at night, her body and her soul yearning for something she told herself she didn't want.

But she did. Oh, God, she did. And it scared her. Especially as the most she'd seen of him had been in passing and then briefly during a foundation meeting before he'd been paged. His gaze had been hooded and intense when it settled on her, and horror of horrors—she'd fluttered.

She still wanted Adam with an intensity that made her ache.

And she was lonely, dammit. When she'd never been lonely for a man before.

Glancing at her desk monitor, she was surprised to find it was nearly seven o'clock. Reaching up to remove the hairpins digging into her scalp, she shook her hair free and sank her fingers into the heavy mass to give her beleaguered scalp a good massage. Closing her eyes in relief, she let out a long sigh and sank back in her chair only to jolt upright when a familiar voice drawled, "Finally letting your hair down?"

Her pulse jumped and her darned heart fluttered at the sight of the man she'd just been fantasizing about lounging in the doorway. He looked even better than she remembered, and for just an instant, she struggled to recall exactly why she was so determined to keep him at arm's length.

"Literally speaking," she murmured, trying not to recall the last time she'd *let her hair down* with him or the way her body began buzzing like she was plugged into a transformer. "It's been a crazy week."

He scrubbed a hand down his face, his rough laugh drawing her sharpening gaze. He was still the hot, hunky Dr. Knight women sighed over, but something was very wrong. She could see it in the bleak amber gaze, the paleness of his normally coppery gold skin stretched tight across high cheekbones and the tension around his mouth.

"Yeah," he rasped, his gaze locked on her with burning intensity. "A bad one too."

Alarmed, Sam straightened in her chair, heart tripping over itself as her planned apology for her behavior slipped away. "What happened?" she asked, her gaze searching his.

For several beats, he stared at her, then his breath escaped in an audible whoosh. "We lost a patient today," he admitted quietly, lifting a hand to rub his chest and then grimacing as though he were in pain.

Alarm morphed into terror.

Lurching to her feet, she rounded her desk, her mind desperately skittering over everything she knew about treating a coronary. If she hadn't panicked in Juniper Falls, she railed at herself, and paid more attention with Gladys, she would know what to do now.

And God, she thought, when the blood drained from her head, she didn't want Adam to die. *Anything...*anything *but that.*

"T-tell me what to d-do," she babbled, grabbing his wrist to search for a pulse and panicking because she couldn't find one. "I can't p-promise not to f-freak out but I'll do exactly as you s-say—"

The next thing she knew Adam grasped her chin in warm fingers and firmly lifted her face to his. "Hey, *hey*," he repeated firmly when her breath hitched on a sob. "Look at me, Samantha. I'm not having a heart attack, if that's what you're thinking."

She froze and stared at him, *her* heart feeling like it was going into spasms and would burst out of her chest any second. Her vision began to fade around the edges.

"*No!*" She shook her head violently, dislodging his touch as she tried to push her hands against his chest right over his heart. "I—I've seen it before and—"

"*Samantha!*" The gentle firmness of his voice finally reached her. She froze as he cupped her face firmly in his hands and gave her a little shake. "Look at me," he ordered softly and waited until her gaze met his before assuring her calmly, "I'm fine. I promise. Now breathe."

She blinked and finally noticed that his skin didn't have the same gray color of Gladys's and Mrs. Hopkins's and his lips weren't blue. Needing something to hold onto, she wrapped her hands around his brawny wrists and focused on his mouth as her world slowly settled.

Finally, she lifted her gaze to search his. "You're—sure?"

He reached out to smooth an unruly lock

of hair behind her ear. "Yeah," he murmured softly. "I'm sure. It's just—" He sucked air into his lungs and tugged her against him, wrapping her up in his embrace and burying his face in her hair.

Shocked by the move—the raw emotion in his voice—Sam could only slide her arms around him and press her body close in an instinctive need to offer comfort. She was glad of the support too since her knees wobbled alarmingly.

"It's just what?" she murmured, her throat working furiously as she burrowed close.

His big body shuddered and he tightened his hold, pulling her impossibly closer. "It was a long shot but we were hoping—" He broke off and sighed.

"I'm sorry," she offered lamely, turning her face into his throat to press her lips against his warm skin. "I know how awful it can be. It's terrifying having someone's life in your hands. I don't know how you handle that every day." She pulled back a couple of inches to look up at him, experiencing an odd little thrill that he would seek her out when devastated by a loss.

He gently nudged her back and took her hand, guiding her to the desk.

"Something happened, didn't it?" he asked quietly, sitting on the edge and pulling her between his legs, his hands a warm weight on her hips. "Is that why you didn't follow the rest of the family into medicine?"

Damn. The last thing she wanted was to re-hash old demons. But then maybe he deserved to know after talking her down from not one but three freak-outs. It was her turn to sigh as she slid her hands up his muscled arms to his shoulders, forgetting that she'd told him not a week ago that nothing had changed.

Everything had changed; she was just terrified of what it meant.

"I was ten," she admitted with a ragged laugh, abruptly turning sideways in his arms so she didn't have to look at him when she confessed her deepest darkest secret. "My parents had died about a year earlier in an accident and we were already living with my grandmother," she said quietly, thinking back on those awful years. "My brother and sister were rarely home because being much older, they were already in med school. Grandmother often went out at night and I was left alone with the housekeeper. Anyway—" she sucked in a shuddery breath before continuing "—one night Mrs. Hopkins had a h-heart attack. A huge storm had knocked out the power lines and I'd hidden in my closet with a flashlight. I expected her to come and find me and when she didn't, I went downstairs and f-found her—on the kitchen floor." She realized she was holding her breath and exhaled on a rush. "If—if I hadn't been afraid of the dark, I might have been able to save her."

"You were a kid," he reminded her gently. "What about 911?"

She shook her head. "Because of the storm, they took almost two hours to arrive. I s-spent almost two hours alone with—" She broke off and shuddered at the memory.

"With a dead body," he finished quietly, tugging her closer. She nodded and rested her head on his shoulder, glad of its solidity and width.

"Yes."

"Hell," he cursed on an explosive exhale. "No wonder you have panic attacks. It would have traumatized anyone, let alone a ten-year-old."

"I'm not ten anymore, Adam," she said tiredly.

"Yeah," he murmured, turning her into his arms. Sliding his hand beneath her hair, he tipped her face to his, eyes gleaming with warm amusement as he slid his lips along her jaw to her ear. "I noticed." She shivered and arched her neck to give him more room, enjoying his warmth and strength. "Fears don't always make sense, Sam, but everyone has them."

"I can't see you letting some childhood trauma paralyze you," she murmured, sliding her hands up his hard abdomen and melting inside when the flesh beneath bunched and rippled.

"You'd be surprised," he growled, brushing his lips against the pulse in her throat that felt like it bumped against her skin, yearning to get closer. "The thought of asking you on a date terrifies me."

She stilled as the words registered and he took the opportunity to nip her jaw. "A d-date?" she squeaked moving back to gape at him, unsure why she was so shocked by the concept of a date. With Adam.

"Yeah," he murmured with a soft chuckle. "We've done things a little backward. So, what do you say to dinner and—" He paused, a look of annoyed resignation passing across his features, and it was then that Sam realized the buzzing she felt where their bodies were pressed together had nothing to do with sexual tension vibrating between them.

With a heavy sigh, Adam silenced his pager. Instead of moving away, he tightened his arms around her and dropped his forehead to hers. "Looks like our date will have to wait," he murmured softly, and Sam had to squeeze her eyes closed so he didn't see her disappointment.

Damn. Since when had she been yearning for something as simple as a date?

"Looks like," she agreed, the tightness in her throat way out of proportion to the situation. They didn't know each other well enough for her to feel the loss even before he left to attend to his patients. As though something deep within her needed to cling to this new closeness between them, the unfamiliar emotions flooding her that went beyond the physical. It should have terrified the woman who'd learned early on to hide her emotions from a grandmother who'd neither the patience nor the empathy for a little girl who'd been torn from everything familiar.

It did terrify her, she admitted silently, but not as much as the knowledge that he might not feel the same way. Because it meant that despite her plans, despite her recent experiences, she was headed for heartbreak that made Lawrence's betrayal feel like nothing more than disillusionment in someone she'd thought she'd known.

This close, she couldn't hide the tremor that went through her and when he wrapped a warm hand around her neck and tipped up her chin, the query in his warm whiskey gaze had her lashes sweeping down to hide the prick of tears that surprised as well as baffled her.

"Hey," he murmured softly, bending his knees to frown into her eyes. "You okay?" So much for hiding her emotions.

Sam gave a watery laugh and pushed away from him when all she wanted to do was cling. "I'm fine." Without looking at him, she patted his chest absently and moved behind her desk, abruptly needing space to think about the emotions currently tying her in intricate knots. "Go use your superpowers, Dr. Knight, while I use mine to see how much money I can make for your foundation."

He was silent a long moment, and when she sneaked a peek at him, he was studying her intently, his mouth somber, eyes unreadable. "This won't take long and we'll—"

"Adam," she interrupted softly. God, she needed him to go before she embarrassed herself. "It's okay. We'll make plans for the next time you're not on call and *I'm* not crazy busy with the gallery evening." He opened his mouth just as his pager buzzed again. "Go," she laughingly ordered when he spun away with an impatient growl and headed for the door. "I have work to do."

When he got to the door, he planted one hand on the frame and sent her a heated look over his broad shoulder. "This discussion isn't over," he promised, his voice deep and rough with just a hint of warning that sent caution twisting up her spine. "I shouldn't be long. We can have a late dinner."

She waited until she heard the outer door close before sinking into the chair, her breath an audible whoosh in the silence. Her knees wobbled and her hands shook, her heart thundering in her ears.

"What the heck was that?" she demanded, when she was very much afraid she already knew. Her emotions were rapidly becoming difficult to ignore. Adam though? Who knew what he thought, how he felt about anything, especially her. But then again, hadn't she constantly told him he was a rebound and that she had a plan for her life? A life that didn't include him?

Of course, he wouldn't verbalize his feelings when he found so many similarities between his mother and Sam. And he was determined not to become like his father, which meant he'd never let himself feel anything deeper for her than hot lust and mild affection.

Pressing the heel of her hand to the pinch beside her heart, Sam shut down her computer and tidied her desk. She would go home, pour herself a glass of wine and pretend that her life wasn't spiraling out of control. She would pretend that being judged by someone else's actions didn't shred her heart and she wouldn't let herself be devastated when Adam grew tired of her inconsistent behavior and moved on.

Because he would. She wasn't gorgeous and exciting like the women he probably usually dated and she was too old to wait around for someone too busy living for other people. She'd waited for Lawrence to find time to be with her, to love her, she realized with a flash of insight. As though she hadn't deserved more. She was done with that.

But could she believe that Adam really wanted something as simple as a date when they'd already done so much more? And if so, why?

Why now?

And why the heck did it matter so much?

Sam had been asleep for only a short while when she heard pounding. She tried to turn over and pull a pillow over her head but it didn't shut out the noise. Finally, with a sigh, she got up because the crazy person clearly wasn't going away and she didn't want the noise waking her neighbors.

She opened the door to find Adam, hands shoved into his jeans pockets, leaning against the wall, looking hot and brooding, and more than a little dangerous. In an instant, her exhaustion and depression vanished.

For long tense moments, they stared at each other while her jittering pulse jerked, stumbled and then took up a slow sluggish rhythm. The last thing she'd expected when she'd left the office was that he'd follow—especially after her embarrassing meltdown. She'd admitted more to him than the therapist she'd seen as a child.

His thick hair shone blue-black beneath the

overhead light, his chiseled features seemingly cast in granite. Eyes, hooded and slumberous, gleamed like light-shot bourbon between his sooty lashes making it difficult to interpret his thoughts.

Struggling against the conflicting emotions she had no idea how to handle, Sam was tempted to slam and lock the door before she did something stupid. Like yank him inside so she could get her hands and mouth all over him.

"Dr. Knight," she said breathlessly, her fingers tightening on the door because she'd discovered that she was achingly vulnerable when it came to this man and her instinct was to protect herself.

Her formality had one eyebrow rising up his forehead to disappear into the lock of hair that refused to be tamed. *Kind of like him*, she thought. Kind of like the way he made her feel.

"Miss Jefferies," he drawled with an ironic twist of his lips. He hadn't moved but she could feel the pull of his magnetism and it scared as much as it excited her. "You opened the door without checking the peephole," he accused, his voice a rough slide of velvet against her skin.

"You're the only crazy person I know who likes to wake people up in the middle of the night," she said, wildly pleased that she managed to sound coolly amused and thought, *Oh, look, I learned something useful from Lilian after all.*

His gaze drilled into hers and after a couple of silent beats, he pushed away from the wall to crowd her in the open doorway. Her heart bumped against her ribs and her breath backed up in her lungs, everything within her stilling at the crackling tension he brought with him. And suddenly channeling Grandma Lilian fizzled like a wet cracker.

Dammit, the man was too potent for her own good.

"Yeah, crazy," he murmured, his deep sinful voice wrapping her in heady sensations. When she refused to move, he placed a large palm against her belly and gently propelled her backward into her condo.

She didn't resist because the awful truth was she was emotionally attached in a way she'd never been before and was afraid it was deep and permanent. But she couldn't think about that right now, not when he'd crowded her against the small foyer desk with his big warm body.

Staring up into his boldly handsome face, she couldn't help noticing how the warm glow from the sitting room lamps slanted across his features and threw them into stark relief. The shimmer of light through his remarkable eyes took her breath away, watching her with predatory intent and more than a little impatience.

She curled her fingers around the edge of

the desk, hoping the sharp pain would keep her grounded. But then he slowly leaned forward and the breath backed up in her throat. Anticipation ratcheted up a thousand notches and just when she thought he'd kiss her—her lips had parted on a soft anticipatory gasp—he angled his head to brush his mouth against her ear, tugging a gasp from her lips, before dropping to press an open-mouthed kiss against her throat.

"You left," he murmured before sucking a small patch of sensitized skin into his mouth. Her breath hitched as her mouth opened but all that emerged was a strangled laugh.

"You expected me to…to wait?" she finally demanded, the query morphing into a startled squeak at the tiny punishing nip he inflicted on the muscle joining her neck and shoulder.

"Why not?" he growled, nudging her thighs apart and pressing up against her heated core, covered in the thinnest stretchy lace. "I've waited a lifetime for you. But I'm done waiting, Samantha."

Before she could ask what he meant, Adam took her mouth greedily, his hands filling with her breasts, and when her head finally cleared enough to recall those words, his big body was sprawled across hers in exhaustion.

CHAPTER ELEVEN

SAM REARRANGED THE remaining canapés on the platter to make room for a new batch as the servers rushed around her. Fine wine and conversation flowed freely in the art gallery she'd managed to charm into hosting the charity event, along with artworks donated by local artists. The caterers she'd hired were worth every dollar they were charging and the evening was to all intents and purposes a huge success.

So what the heck are you doing hiding out in the kitchen when the results of all your hard work are out there?

She paused and thrust out her bottom lip to blow cool air into her hot face. She should be reveling in her success. Instead, she was hiding in the kitchen, hoping no one would notice she was having a breakdown. Because that's exactly how she'd felt ever since Adam had uttered those cryptic words, stolen her breath along with her mind and then fallen asleep.

That was two days ago.

Two days since she'd heard his pager go off; two days since he'd grunted irritably as he'd rolled away from her and she'd curled around his pillow to hold his heat to her a little longer. Exhausted, she'd been vaguely aware of him smoothing the hair off her cheek with a gentle hand before kissing her softly.

"Gotta go," he'd murmured against her mouth between kisses, and when she'd moaned and let her lips cling sleepily to his, she thought he'd murmured something that sounded like, "We can't go on like this, Sam. We need to talk," but she must have dreamed it because other than a bouquet of wildflowers that had appeared on her desk the following day without a card—from Adam?—she hadn't so much as received a call or text message from him.

There'd been no talking and things had gone on exactly as they had. One of them disappearing after a hot night of sex and then…*nothing*.

Or maybe—maybe he'd been kissing her off. Had the flowers and the cryptic message been his way of saying they were done? Is that what he'd meant by *we can't go on like this*?

She had no idea and the suspense was killing her.

Fortunately, organizing tonight's event had kept her too busy to obsess and she'd managed to push everything firmly to the back of her mind. Until *he'd* arrived, looking Hollywood handsome in a dark designer suit over a white T-shirt that emphasized his tall rangy build, overlong inky hair and coppery gold skin. It had also emphasized the glowing amber eyes that reminded her of a large mountain cat lying in wait.

Like a besotted adolescent, she'd known the instant he'd arrived by the shiver that had raised the hairs on the back of her neck. Engaged in a spirited debate about the stereotypical views that persisted in discussions on Native American art, Sam had looked up and locked gazes with him. That seemingly endless moment of connection had sent a wave of heat and longing storming through her and she'd promptly forgotten what she was saying.

In truth, it had lasted only a second before he was swamped like a celebrity, and she'd been left feeling hollow and alone in a roomful of people. A feeling so common that she'd run and hidden. It was mortifying to discover that she was still that insecure little girl desperate to belong. It made her angry and emotionally raw.

Fine, she admitted, thrusting out her bottom lip and exhaling explosively. It was seeing him surrounded by all those beautiful women that had all her insecurities swamping her. *God*. She wished she had more experience on how to handle these kinds of situations but she was an emotional coward; preferring to lock down her emotions. And hide.

Besides, did she go out there and demand to know what he'd meant or pretend that everything was fine? Pretend that seeing Tiffany Travers, legendary man-eater and celebrity tech-heiress, wrapped around him like Christmas ribbon didn't send shards of hurt and anger ripping through her?

Or did she—?

"Darling, what on earth are you doing hiding in here?" Aunt Coco's voice jolted Sam rudely out of her silent self-debate. "Are you all right?"

Hastily composing herself, Sam turned with a smile she hoped appeared genuine. "Of course I am," she assured the older woman. It wouldn't do to let the other woman know just how ragged her nerves were or *worse*—why. "Have you seen all those red stickers? I don't think there's one item left for sale."

"I have and I also know that the caterers are excellent and can handle everything in here," Coco said. "Now come, everyone's asking for you."

"In a minute," Sam promised a bit vaguely. "It's been so insane the past week. I just need a quiet moment."

Aunt Coco frowned and after a couple of

beats, reached out to cup Sam's face between her elegant hands. "You look unhappy," she murmured, studying Sam with gentle intensity that had Sam wishing she were better at hiding her feelings. "You've been quiet and withdrawn the last few days. Are you regretting moving here and taking over the foundation?"

"Oh, no," Sam hastened to assure the older woman. "Not at all." That was the one thing she didn't regret. "I'm enjoying the challenge. It's much more rewarding than babysitting artwork and I like feeling that I'm helping make a difference."

"You are, but I can't help but think that I've made a mess of things by encouraging you to break away from Lilian."

"You haven't," she insisted firmly, giving Coco a quick hug. Leaving Boston was the best thing she could have done. "And I'm not unhappy. It's just a headache, that's all." Yeah, he was a *big* headache. Then because she needed to stop thinking about him, she said, "In fact, I'm really glad we've had a chance to reconnect. I missed you and grandpa."

"And we missed you, darling," Coco murmured, her green eyes misting with tears. "You are *so* like him, you know. Sweet and caring and so full of life and vitality. With your gentle nature, we were worried Lilian would crush you."

"She nearly succeeded," Sam muttered, ashamed to recall all the times she'd buckled to her grandmother's dictates, giving in rather than fighting for her own identity.

"I couldn't be happier that you accepted the job. For me, for the foundation and for—Adam."

Sam stilled a moment, then returned her attention to arranging canapés, hoping that Aunt Coco bought the casual move, knowing she wasn't fooling anyone. "Adam?"

There was a short pause before Coco's softly chiding voice said, "I know you and I know Adam, sweetheart. Something happened in Juniper Falls that's making you unhappy."

"Nothing happened," she lied, desperate for it to be true. "And I'm just tired. *Really*. The past two weeks have been hectic with all the details for tonight." She sent Aunt Coco a preoccupied smile she hoped the other woman bought. "I wanted this evening to be a success."

"Well, it certainly is that," Coco said with a chuckle. "In fact, we're all in agreement that this should become an annual event. With a little more time, I'm positive you could badger even more artists into contributing. You're doing a wonderful job, just as I predicted. I couldn't be prouder of you."

She reached out and hugged Sam. "Oh," she said archly as she released her. "And just in case you were wondering, Tiffany Travers came with Paul Gilberts and abandoned him the instant she saw Adam arrive alone. She's been after him since before her divorce." She paused as though to let her words sink in before continuing. "Are you going to let her get her hooks in your man?"

Sam's startled gaze jumped to Coco's. "He's n-not *mine*," she protested quickly, ignoring the sudden pressure in her chest that felt very much like panic, especially when Coco's eyebrow arched. "Really, Aunt Coco, *nothing* happened." Well, nothing other than a few hot nights of sex—and maybe a looming heartbreak for her.

Coco cocked her head and studied Sam in a way that made her nervous. Casually turning away from that shrewd glance, she reached for the container of canapés.

"Does this have something to do with your plan?" Coco demanded, clearly not done.

"What plan?" she asked absently.

"That ridiculous life plan you concocted," Coco said briskly. "The one that stops you from throwing caution to the wind and grabbing life with both hands."

"That's not why—"

"Adam is not Lawrence," Coco interrupted smartly, clearly not done having her say. "He would never have a relationship based on lies and deceit. He values family more than anyone I know. He's fiercely loyal and feels deeply even if he'd like to deny it." She sighed, cupping Sam's face. "Oh, darling, that plan isn't you. What happened to emotion and joy? Whatever happened to spontaneity and taking a risk on life and love?"

Sam's eyes widened at the woman's vehemence. "Love?" she gasped, appalled. "Aunt Coco—"

"Dammit, I could shake you," the other woman snapped. "Your grandfather would be ashamed of you for being such a coward."

Coming on the heels of her own self-flagellation, the accusation stung and Sam took a step back only to ram her hip into the counter behind her. She sucked in a sharp painful breath and curled her fingers around the edge to steady herself. "C-coward?"

Oh, damn. Did Coco know she still had panic attacks and avoided anything that would cause them? Did she see the pain and panic threatening to break her apart inside at the thought of Adam moving on to someone like Tiffany Travers—or one of the other gorgeous, sophisticated women surrounding him?

"Yes," Coco affirmed firmly, and for an instant, Sam wondered if she'd spoken out loud. "For hiding and ignoring what's in front of your nose." And with that parting shot, she spun away and left Sam gaping at her retreating back, too shocked to admit that she hadn't thought of her plan in weeks.

"You okay, Ms. Jefferies?" the head server enquired.

She nodded quickly, embarrassed that anyone had heard her being called a coward. "I'm fine," she said firmly, returning to the job she was making a complete hash of when he looked unconvinced. "Rough day."

Hell, rough year. But she would be fine, she vowed fiercely. Soon. Maybe. All she had to remember was that she wasn't the kind of woman to inspire grand passion or loyalty in men and she'd be fine. Lawrence, whom she'd known most of her life, had been promised the position of CEO of Gilford Pharmaceuticals once Lilian retired if he married her and had been quite happy to live a lie to gain access to the Gilford billions. She felt like a complete idiot for not seeing that sooner. *Or* that he was gay.

Adam? Well, who knew what motivated him? Because she had no idea. Maybe the gossip was right. Maybe he had a thing for socialites—a very *temporary* thing that allowed him to exorcise his demons without engaging his heart.

Scowling at the platter, she forcibly moved a couple of canapés. Not that *she* was a socialite. Far from it. She'd always had a job, wasn't exactly known for being fashionable and was rarely seen at the "right" parties with the "right" people.

As much as she hated to admit it, she was more Samantha than Amanda. Amanda was fun and spontaneous, full of courage and vitality. Amanda was sexy and exciting while Samantha was…*meh*. She was bland, uninteresting and—*bleh*.

Was it any wonder, she asked herself when she returned to the party and immediately caught sight of Adam, head bent intimately toward Tiffany and laughing as they shared a joke, that he would prefer being in the company of gorgeous, exciting women?

Ignoring the knife-sharp pain spearing through her body, she spun away only to lurch into someone right behind her. She stumbled back a step, an automatic apology on her lips.

"Oh," she gasped when she saw exactly who it was. Her heart sank. The last time she'd seen Blake Lowry had been their dinner date where he'd hinted that a donation came with a price. A price she wasn't prepared to pay.

"Mr. Lowry. I—I'm sorry, I didn't see you."

"Samantha," Blake Lowry drawled smoothly. He lifted his wine glass and took a sip of excellent Zinfandel, his eyes glittering as they swept over her in a way that made her uncomfortable. "I thought you'd agreed to call me Blake?"

"Yes, of course," she said graciously, pasting on her social smile as she edged away under the guise of facing him. Blake Lowry, it seemed, thought every woman was flattered by his attention, one of those obnoxious men who thought their money and social status gave them permission to take what—and whom—they wanted, regardless. "Have you tried the lobster rolls or the salmon and watercress wraps? The caterer's recipe is—"

"As excellent as they are," he drawled, lifting his hand to brush intimately at a tendril of hair that had escaped her updo. "I'm not interested in swapping recipes, Samantha."

"What about the artwork?" she asked, dislodging his hand by turning to the large painting of the New Mexico landscape beside them. "I noticed earlier that you were interested in the sculpture. Have you met the artist?"

His eyes dropped to her breasts and she had to force herself not to recoil, reminded that she was more than adequately covered—in the front, at least. "I'm much more interested in why you've been avoiding me."

"Not at all," she said sweetly. "As hostess, I've been busy and—"

"Too busy to spend time with a potential donor?" he interrupted softly, catching her hand and tucking it into the crook of his arm. Sam's instinct was to snatch her hand away but she resisted the urge, especially when he tightened his grip on her fingers. What she couldn't stop, however, was the irritation that stiffened her spine.

"Of course not," she said graciously, all but gritting her teeth. "I—"

"I'm delighted to hear it," he interrupted again, much to Sam's growing annoyance. He'd done that during their dinner too, reminding her that he was the kind of man who wasn't interested in anything a woman had to say, only that she made him look good. "Why don't you tell me more about your little foundation while we admire the artwork?"

Adam looked down at Tiffany Travers, who was practically bonded to his side, and wondered how he was going to pry her off without causing a scene. For years, petite blondes had kind of been his type—a shrink would have a field day with that, considering his mother was one—but now all he could hear was the sound of husky laughter drifting over the noise of the crowd. Husky laughter that had the power to make him smile even when he didn't feel like smiling.

Especially as she was purposely avoiding him; which made as little sense as the emotion he'd caught in her expressive eyes before her public mask had slipped into place. As a foundation board member, he was forced to play the social game when all he wanted was to hunt her down and demand to know what game *she* was playing.

Watching her out of the corner of his eye while pretending interest in the conversation around him, Adam decided that dealing with Samantha was like tracking the elusive spotted lynx. As frustrating as it was, those rare glimpses he had only made him more determined to catch her.

Her back was to him and the sight of her long slender, *naked* spine had his blood pressure hiking to dangerous heights. And not in a good way. Especially with pretty boy's hand straying to the dip in her waist just above the shallow dimples at the base of her spine. He wanted to march over there and physically remove the offending touch but since she didn't seem to mind, he couldn't very well toss her over his shoulder and drag her into his cave like a Neanderthal.

He wanted to publicly claim her as his but he was all too aware that she'd chosen the golden god with his casually tousled blond hair, careful bronzed tan and elegantly expensive suit. Teamed with the effortless confidence the social elite seemed to be born with, it identified him as someone who'd grown up in the same world as Samantha. Together, they drew the eye, standing out among the other couples filling the gallery. Smooth, polished with the kind of class that shouted money—and lots of it.

It was something Adam would never have and could never offer Samantha. Not the billions her family was reputed to be worth. He was who he was and he'd long since come to terms with it. Living in San José, rubbing shoulders with the upper classes and dating socialites would never make him one of them and he was fooling himself if he thought he had anything to offer Samantha other than the brutal hours of a busy surgeon.

None of that seemed to matter, however, because the sight of another man touching places where Adam's lips had been was eliciting some pretty fierce emotions that smacked of jealousy. Since he'd never been jealous over a woman before, the roiling emotions were as unwelcome as they were unexpected.

Which is probably why he stayed where he was surrounded by women he had little interest in while visually tracking Sam's movements and tracing the delicate line of her spine, the pale creamy skin between the wide V of silver-shot black. Most of the women present were dressed far more provocatively than Samantha, but none of them looked as sexy or classy.

With determined effort, he tried to ignore the swirl of anger and confusion, and focus on Tiffany's high titters and breathless account of her week in Cabo San Lucas. Frankly, he couldn't have cared less about her topless bathing or the new micro bikini she was offering to model for him.

All he could think about was watching the guy dip his head to whisper something in Sam's ear. All he could wonder was if she was shivering the way she did when Adam kissed the soft skin beneath that same ear. And all he could imagine was punching the guy in his perfect nose.

Damn the stuffed shirt for looking like he was anticipating molding Samantha into something as erotic as the sculpture they were studying, he thought with a burst of fury as the guy suddenly tugged her toward the dark hallway that probably led to the owner's offices. Empty and quiet this time of night.

Abruptly excusing himself, Adam ignored Tiffany's shocked protest and wended his way between the wine-guzzling crowd discussing everything from the San José Sharks' recent win to the price of tech stocks.

With his gaze locked where he'd last seen Samantha, Adam didn't stop until he stepped into the passage, just in time to hear a husky voice say, "Mr. Lowry—Blake, stop. As flattered as I am by your offer, I really need to get back and…*oh!*"

Adam heard a faint scuffle, an outraged squeak and took a couple of long strides down the darkened passage, arriving in time to see Samantha pinned against the wall, trying to avoid the man's hands and mouth.

By the time he reached them, Samantha's dress had been ripped off one smooth shoulder and the guy's hand was up her skirt.

"Blake, *stop*."

Her shocked squeak had fury exploding through Adam's skull, and before he knew he'd moved, he'd grabbed the other man and flung him against the opposite wall. After one quick glance at Samantha's shocked face, he turned to face Lowry, taking care to block her body with his.

"I distinctly heard the lady say stop," he drawled, tamping down the fury that darkened the edges of his vision. If there was one thing he hated, it was men forcing themselves on unwilling women.

"Who the *hell* are you?" the man demanded, looking furious at the interruption. With a jerk, he adjusted the jacket Adam had practically ripped off him and smoothed his hair back into its preppy neatness.

"A witness if Miss Jefferies decides to press charges," he said, ignoring Sam's soft moan of humiliation.

"Charges?" the guy drawled, one eyebrow arching arrogantly as he flicked imaginary lint off his jacket sleeve. "For what exactly?"

"Assault," Adam snapped coldly, his eyes narrowing dangerously as the other man began to laugh, gaze scathing as it swept over Adam.

"You seriously think anyone's going to believe the word of a redskin over *me*?" His insulting emphasis reminded Adam of all the times he'd been called redskin and half-breed. "Do you know who I am, *Tonto*?"

Adam's muscles hardened, and as though she knew he was imagining lashing out at the man's smug face, Sam grabbed hold of his jacket. "Please, Adam," she murmured, tightening her grip. "Let it go." And when he and the other man continued their stare-down, she rasped in a low intense voice, "*Please*."

After a tense silence, Blake gave a bark of mocking laughter, his gaze flicking over Sam with insulting lewdness. "You're welcome to her, Cochise," he drawled insolently, pushing away from the wall where he'd been lounging. "Mousy ice queens aren't my thing anyway, but it was fun seeing if I could get her to melt."

With a contemptuous smirk that said, *My proposition still stands, babe. Let me know if you're willing to trade a nice chunk of change for your little charity,* Blake Lowry turned and sauntered off, leaving a tense silence in his wake.

Furious that she would put up with being mauled and insulted by a smug, arrogant jerk because of his money and social standing, Adam spun around abruptly, forcing her to release her grip on him. Startled by his abrupt move, she backed away, looking wide-eyed and wary. Not that he could blame her since aggression pumped hot and fierce through his veins.

Unable to help himself, he raked his gaze across her disheveled appearance, taking in the way her dress sagged on one side, exposing a pale shoulder and the tempting swell of her breast. Her elegantly upswept hair looked a little mussed and Adam hated that the other man had seen her like this—soft and tousled and anything but ice-queenly.

Fury rolled through him again.

After a long pause, he lifted a hand to slide the dress back over her shoulder with fingers that shook.

A visible tremor moved through her as her head jerked up, her eyes wide and liquid as their gazes locked. Suppressed emotion darkened her eyes and one lone drop of liquid clung to her lashes. The sight of it tilted the earth on its axis and something clenched hard in his chest.

Feeling abruptly off balance, he fisted shaking

hands and shoved them into his trouser pockets to prevent himself from reaching for her. "You okay?" he rasped, telling himself fiercely that nothing had changed. When suddenly *everything* had.

Seeing her in her social element among other beautiful people had brought home to him how little he had to offer her. He refused to be like his father and he'd been kidding himself thinking there could be a future for them. He didn't fit into her world any more than she fitted into his and he'd be damned if he'd beg.

Her throat worked spasmodically before her voice emerged low and husky as she said, "I'm fine...thank you," in a tone so polite his jaw clenched.

And because he felt as though his life were spinning out of control, he gave a brief nod and walked away before the crushing need to yank her into his arms and beg her to love him overwhelmed his common sense.

CHAPTER TWELVE

As Adam walked away—the expression in his suddenly remote eyes telling her this was the last time—Samantha blinked back the burn of tears and pressed a hand to the cramping in her belly.

Her breath escaped in a long shudder as she sank back against the wall, grateful for the support, the moment of solitude. The relief, however, was short-lived as nausea abruptly rose, sending her rushing into the bathroom.

Fortunately, she was alone when she burst into the ladies' room, heading for the nearest stall where she promptly lost the contents of her stomach. Not that there was much to lose, she thought with a grimace. Confrontation had always made her feel sick but Blake's attack— and Adam's awful remoteness—left her shaking so hard she could barely stand. How did other women handle such situations? And why had Adam reacted as he had?

Staggering from the stall, she caught sight of

her reflection in the vanity mirror and froze. Her eyes were huge, stark in her pasty white face and a sheen of perspiration dotted her brow. She looked like she would fly apart at the seams at the slightest encouragement.

It was at that moment she saw herself clearly for the first time. And what she saw had anger abruptly flashing through her, snapping her spine straight and flooding her cheeks with color.

Blake was right, dammit, she thought with a rush of self-loathing. He was a bigoted ass, true, but he was right. About her, at least. She *was* a mouse and it was time she became a lioness— like the rest of the women in her family.

She was a Jefferies and a Gilford. Her mother—who'd defied Lilian Gilford to study medicine and marry a doctor with no pedigree— would be ashamed of the woman she'd become. Heck, *she* was ashamed of the woman she'd become. No wonder her grandmother had found it so easy to manipulate her into a relationship with Lawrence.

She was a wimp and it was time she grew into her own woman.

Hands shaking, she stomped over to the basin and glared at the woman reflected there. "I'm done," she told her reflection fiercely. Done being a mouse and she was done being *meh*.

Ripping off a section of paper towel, she

dampened it and began to pat her face. For heaven's sake, she looked like she'd been dragged through a hedge backward. If she was going out there, she was going to do it armored, she told herself firmly.

She'd repair her flawless makeup and pretend she had her life together. She'd march out there and demand to know what Adam had meant when he'd sent her flowers after saying they needed to talk. He'd left in the middle of the night; he'd kissed her as though he'd wanted to slide back against her body—and then nothing.

Not a phone call or even a text message. And dammit, she deserved to know why he constantly blew hot, then cold. The stress was killing her, tying her stomach into knots. If he told her they were finished, she'd face the heartbreak with cool dignity.

Or pretend anyway, because the Gilford and Jefferies women were tigresses.

With anger and a new determination fueling her, Sam repaired her appearance and left the bathroom only to discover that Adam had already left.

Dammit, she thought, stewing, you'd think he'd at least have the courtesy of cooperating when she finally had her "moment of truth." What the heck was she to do with all this roiling determination and energizing anger if she had no one to direct it at?

Fortunately, Blake Lowry had also left because with Adam gone, Sam had been tempted to hunt down the smug bastard and punch him in the face for the racist insults he'd aimed at Adam. And another one for attacking her.

Aunt Coco offered to help with the cleanup but Sam sent her home. Coco may not look it but she was nearly seventy. Besides, left to thank their guests and handle cleanup meant she had no time to focus on her problems or the crushing disappointment and looming heartbreak.

It was only on her way home that she suddenly recalled Adam's expression as he'd turned away and stomped off. There'd been something fierce and hot in his eyes and she wanted to know what it was. Even if it meant that expression had been anger directed at her, she wanted him to look her in the eye and tell her she was a mess he wanted no part of.

She tried calling him once she got home but his phone was off, and despite waiting all night for him to return her call, her phone remained stubbornly silent. At dawn, she dressed and headed to the hospital, determined to catch him before he went into surgery only to discover that he'd taken a leave of absence and left town.

Stunned, Sam shut herself in her office and

pretended to work all the while wondering what the hell had happened. Aunt Coco left a message that she'd be in hospital board meetings the entire day and Sam couldn't pretend she wasn't relieved. She wasn't up to dealing with questions or the other woman's shrewdly perceptive gaze.

She was wired and looked awful—as if she hadn't slept in days and was subsisting on caffeine. It was hard enough convincing herself she was fine without having to actually face Coco.

It was only when she got home that night and switched on the news that she realized where Adam had gone. The Sierras was burning and Juniper County was directly in destruction's path. She might be mad at Adam but he wasn't the kind of man to lie on a beach somewhere while his hometown was in danger.

For several long minutes, the images flashing across the screen held Sam spellbound with horror. Towering flames, fed by the hot air rushing up from the south east, greedily swept across the mountains, consuming everything in their path.

She'd seen television footage of wildfires before, but never when she'd been personally invested in the victims. She knew them and it was horrifying.

Cell-phone footage showed people risking their lives to save their animals; long lines of firefighters clearing fire control lines; specialized vehicles digging dozer lines in the vain hopes of containing the blaze; and people watching helplessly as their properties went up in flames.

The reporter said trained personnel were stretched thin and the local Incident Command Center was calling for volunteers even as smoke jumpers from all over the world began converging on the Sierras. It was a desperate attempt to save people's homes, their livelihoods caught in the wildfire's path.

Even before she'd realized she'd made a decision, Sam was reaching for her phone. Adam had flown into danger to help the people of Juniper Falls. The hospital and Leah were in peril, as were Gladys and Ida—along with all their friends and family. They needed help.

Maybe she couldn't fight the fire or help the injured, but she was an ace at organization and she had a ton of contacts. Juniper Falls needed help and she was going to get it for them.

Adam drove through the darkness, his eyes gritty with fatigue. He'd gone nearly three days without sleep and it was beginning to tell—slowing down his reflexes. *Dammit*, he thought, wrenching at the wheel as he struggled to keep his vehicle on the road, he'd better pay attention before the wind blew him off the pass.

Coming around that last bend, he'd barely

missed a family of black bears walking in the middle of the road. To the east, a smoky red glow illuminated the night sky and every few miles he had to slam on the brakes to avoid the animals fleeing the approaching inferno. He'd already seen so many charred remains that he'd probably have nightmares for years.

He'd been closer to those flames than he'd liked and would never forget the sound of them chewing up his cousin's ranch. That jet engine roar would stay with him for the rest of his life— as would the heat and the smell of burnt, devastated landscape.

His cousin was lucky to be alive and had his ranch hands to thank for yanking him to safety. In the chaos of trying to save his horses, Ben had fallen into a gulley, broken his leg and given himself concussion, a dislocated shoulder and minor burns down one side of his body. With Ben in the hospital, it had been up to Adam and the two ranch hands to save what was left of the place and retrieve the scattered horses.

The house, mostly built of stone, had barely escaped the inferno but the stables, barn and bunkhouse were burnt out shells of still smoking ash. They'd have to rebuild but having the house mostly spared was a small price to pay for maintaining substantial firebreaks and having other measures implemented. Others hadn't been so lucky and Adam had spent the past few days helping the neighbors and providing emergency medical care to those in need.

But the fire was gaining speed and it was heading straight for Juniper Falls. With tourism its main source of income, the townspeople couldn't afford to lose their revenue. Many would probably refuse to be evacuated and the medical center would be overwhelmed. Even without the added danger of being in the path of the fire, they didn't have the facilities, staff or equipment to handle disasters of such magnitude. The only thing he could do now was get them the help they needed.

As though thinking about the medical center was the excuse his exhausted mind was looking for, an image of Samantha popped into his head as vividly as if she were sitting next to him, rumpled and tousled, her beautiful eyes swimming with hurt.

He'd tried not to think about her the past few days, but thoughts of her ambushed him when he least expected it. And each time, it twisted his gut tighter and tighter.

That last night he'd spent with her, he'd had every intention of talking about where their relationship was going—where *he* wanted it to go. Instead, she'd opened her door, looking all sleepy and warm, and he'd completely lost his head. He'd briefly thought they'd wake up together and talk over breakfast but that hadn't happened either.

In the days that followed there'd been one emergency after another and he hadn't been able to get away. What he'd wanted to say couldn't be said over the phone, so he'd waited for the gallery evening with every intention of whisking her away afterward and having their discussion—before they ended up in bed.

It had been all planned out in his head and then—dammit, he still had no idea what had happened. He'd taken one look at her and felt as though he'd been kicked in the chest.

He'd seen her in any number of settings and the pull had been strong but seeing her among San José's rich, social elite had forced him to acknowledge that she was completely out of his league and he was reaching for a beautiful unattainable star.

Elegant and sexy, she'd looked very much in her element, eclipsing many of the other women there. Her animation—and that damned laugh of hers—had drawn not just his but every man's attention in the room. Then she'd turned, their eyes meeting across the room and he'd felt that cool blue gaze like a blow to his soul. The force of it had made him turn away, reeling from the realization that she'd burrowed so far beneath his skin he would never recover once she was gone. Because let's face it, she belonged more in that world than slumming it with the folks of Juniper Falls and a man driven to help others because he felt empty inside.

The shock had been discovering that she filled him—filled all those empty dark and lonely places. When next he'd seen her, she'd been with Lowry, looking like she belonged with the wealthy businessman.

And he'd been gutted.

It had been sheer self-preservation that had kept him from wading through the crowd and snatching her up. Seeing the man's hands on her had had something dark and ugly swamping him. Walking away had been the hardest thing he'd ever done but he'd had to before he said or did something he could never take back. He'd stalked off, fighting a wild need to go back and wipe that look of hurt accusation from her eyes; but knowing she had the power to shred his soul had spurred him to escape.

The call from Ben's ranch hands had been the excuse he'd needed. Racing to his cousin's side had given him the perfect out and seeing the chaos and devastation had pretty much wiped everything else from his mind.

With cell towers down it had only been when he'd reached the outskirts of Fresno on that first medevac that he'd seen the missed calls from Samantha. He'd been about to call her back, his thumb hovering over her number when he'd abruptly shoved the phone back into his pocket.

What the hell was there to say? That he'd followed his father's footsteps by falling for a woman whose world would never accept him? Hell, he thought with a snort, he lived with that kind of prejudice every day, pretending it didn't affect him. Knowing that Samantha could very well be like his mother did affect him and seeing her with Blake Lowry had forced him to acknowledge that he would never fit into her world or her life.

Women like Samantha didn't fall in love and marry someone from the wrong side of the bedsheets or leave their world for his. It wasn't done. His mother—and every debutante he'd ever dated—had made that more than clear. They had wild, exciting flings with bad boys but married their social equals. Equals like his mother's senator husband—and Blake Lowry.

It was time to forget Samantha Jefferies. Forget about how she made him feel. About how something warm and clean grew in his chest when she laughed; how her breath hitched when he kissed the side of her neck—the expression in her eyes after a panic attack. As if she were ashamed of showing her weaknesses.

He rubbed absently at the ache over his heart at the thought of not being around to talk her through an attack. She would face it alone because she hated anyone seeing her vulnerabilities—didn't want to admit that she had any. Men like Blake Lowry would never understand her and never care enough to try.

Dammit, he thought when the ache grew into an actual physical pain. When had she burrowed so far under his skin that the thought of her unhappiness made him want—*need*—to wrap her in his arms, protect her from the world? Slay her dragons?

But she didn't want him to slay her dragons, and after the incident at the art gallery, it was very clear that she didn't want anything from him at all. Hell, she hadn't even been able to look at him.

It wouldn't be easy, he thought as the sign for Juniper Falls was briefly caught in his headlights. Hopefully, by the time he returned to San José, his damn heart accepted that it could never have what it craved.

He rounded the next bend and was forced to slam on the brakes as he came up behind two truckloads of firefighters. Cursing softly, he reminded himself to pay attention or he'd be needing the medical care he was supposed to be giving.

He followed the trucks through town until he was forced to pull to the side of the road as they turned into the hospital parking. Even as he killed the engine, a loud *whop-whop-whop* filled the night air. He looked up as a helo flew overhead, gaining altitude as it banked over the valley and rose up the steep sides of the mountain to disappear over Chapman's Ridge, its searchlights picking up the growing smoke-cloud being pushed north by the wind.

Frowning, he killed the engine and slid from the Jeep. Was the fire closer than he'd thought or had something happened at the hospital, he wondered, as he took off through the trees. Was that the reason for the truckloads of firefighters?

The instant he broke through the trees, he saw that the hospital parking lot had been turned into a fire-and-rescue Incident Command Center, which explained the firefighters. A mobile operations vehicle was parked off to one side of a large marquee and with the area lit up like a carnival, he could make out a volunteer wild-fire-services vehicle along with forestry-and-park-services trucks that had begun to disgorge their cargo.

Several firefighters were helped through the doors of the hospital's small emergency room while others headed toward the long military tent used for rescue operations. A sheriff's department vehicle—blue lights flashing and doors open as though it had just arrived—was parked off to one side. In the open doorway, a uniformed deputy stood talking into a handheld radio, the bursts of static reaching Adam across the distance.

Intending to get information, Adam started toward him just as a figure emerged from the tent and headed straight for the cop. Adam only saw the person from behind but something about the way they walked seemed familiar. So familiar his gut clenched when the cop's eyes took a leisurely journey over the woman, a smile of appreciation lighting his half-illuminated features.

Blinking his gritty eyes, Adam ground his back teeth together, wondering if his mind was playing tricks on him because for one moment there, the woman had reminded him of—

Then she turned her head, the external light spilling across one side of her face. Adam froze in his tracks, his breath backing up as husky laughter drifted lightly in the night air.

What the hell? Samantha?

Even as he watched, the cop accepted something from her, threw back his head and with a laugh, toasted her with what looked like a disposable cup before lifting it to his smiling mouth.

An indefinable host of emotions stormed though Adam, tightening his chest. Disbelief, shock, anger and a whole bunch of others he couldn't seem to get a handle on. The overriding one was the impulse to storm over there and snatch her away from the other man.

What the hell was wrong with him?

And what the hell was she doing here? It was as if thinking about her had conjured her out of thin air. But this Samantha was unlike any he'd ever seen. Dressed in form-fitting jeans and a loose plaid shirt, rolled up to her forearms, her hair carelessly pulled into a messy topknot, she appeared casual and more relaxed than he'd ever seen her in public.

Before he could attempt to sort out his roiling emotions, or march over there and demand to know what the hell she thought she was doing, someone appeared in the hospital entrance to beckon her, interrupting her cozy little chat. The cop straightened at the interruption, an expression of impatience crossing his face, but Samantha was already moving away.

Suddenly, Adam was no longer exhausted. Furious energy surged through him. Eyes locked on her disappearing back, he followed, determined to find out exactly what she thought she was doing. He'd left her safely in San José. What the hell did she—?

A large hand slapped against his chest, bringing him up short. "S'cuse me, bud. Unless you're injured, you can't go in there."

Adam was so intent on following Samantha, he hadn't seen the deputy until he was almost on him. Instead of replying, he looked down at the hand on his chest and for just an instant was tempted to vent all the emotions that had been tearing him up inside for days.

He controlled it—barely—reminding himself that he wouldn't be able to help anyone from lockup.

"I'm a doctor," he said, voice chilly and flat when he had no right to be angry with Samantha or the cop. He'd given up that right the night of the gallery function.

The guy looked him up and down, his expression derisive. Adam knew exactly what he saw. He hadn't slept in nearly three days and it showed. His clothes were rumpled, stained and he couldn't remember the last time he'd eaten.

"Yeah," the deputy snorted, hands on his equipment belt. "And I'm Yosemite Sam, so you can just—"

"Dr. Knight?" A voice gasped behind him, drawing their attention. "Oh, my God, it is you." Adam immediately recognized the nurse hurrying up behind them.

"What is it, Hannah?"

"You couldn't have come at a better time," the

nurse said with a relieved wobble. "I was looking for one of the volunteer medics but you're a godsend."

"What happened?"

"Frank Pearson was just brought in with chest pains and breathing difficulties." She hurried ahead to push open the swing doors. "They've been clearing lines up near Widow's Bend and we're worried it's a coronary."

Instantly forgetting about the deputy, Adam followed the nurse, concern for Frank momentarily replacing his driving need to find Samantha. He blinked gritty eyes as the bright lights and sounds of an active ER assaulted him. It was the busiest he'd ever seen it. Summers could get pretty busy with the tourist season but the place was filled with people. After the past three hours of dark and quiet, it was almost too much for his tired mind to take in.

"He's in the last cubicle," Hannah said when someone called her name, leaving Adam to push past firefighters in full gear to get to the cubicle. Leah was holding the oxygen mask over the clearly distressed man's nose and mouth, attempting to calm him.

Adam barely recognized Frank Pearson. The volunteer was covered in soot, his eyes red-rimmed, looking like any number of the wildfire victims Adam had treated closer to the family ranch. His eyes were squeezed shut and he was struggling to breathe, his features twisted into a grimace as he pressed a balled-up fist to his chest. Beneath the soot, and the oxygen mask, his skin was gray and sweaty.

Adam acknowledged Leah's relieved smile of greeting and casually placed his fingers on the man's left wrist to check his radial pulse. "You don't look so good, Frank," he said, his attention fixed on the man's face. His pulse was ragged and elevated but still strong.

Frank gave a hoarse laugh that morphed into a wheezing cough, his body arching helplessly as he fought for breath. He finally collapsed back against the bed and lifted a shaky hand to pull away the mask. He was sweating profusely. "You're not looking so good yourself, Doc," he wheezed with a chuckle through blueish lips. "City life not treating you so good?"

"Better than you, my friend," Adam smiled, attempting to lighten the tension as he guided the oxygen mask back in place. He turned to Leah. "See if you can find me a spare stethoscope," he said quietly. "And I'd appreciate someone hunting down a clean pair of scrubs. My clothes have been through a lot today."

She nodded and hurried off.

He gently pressed down on Frank's bottom eyelids to check for soot and burns, noting that his lashes and brows were slightly singed. "Keep breathing into that mask, Frank," he murmured calmly. "And just relax. We'll have you feeling better in no time."

"Lorena," Frank gasped, grabbing Adam's wrist. "And…the kids. They…need…me."

Adam gently but firmly replaced the mask. "Yes, they do but you have to breathe, Frank, or Lorena will have both our hides."

"Hurts like I've been kicked in the chest, Doc. Promise you won't let me die."

"You're not gonna die, Frank," one of the other firefighters burst out angrily when Leah reappeared to thrust a stethoscope at Adam. "Dammit, Doc. Tell him."

"Guys," Leah said firmly, taking charge. "He's not going to let Frank die but you need to give him room to work. Why don't you get something to eat and drink? There's plenty in the tent outside. We'll take care of Frank." She waited until they stepped out of the cubicle before asking, "Adam, what do you need?"

"How's the lab situation?" he asked, fitting the stethoscope earpieces into his ears. He was fairly certain Frank was suffering nothing more than smoke inhalation but a few blood tests would confirm his suspicions. The student doctor gave a small headshake. "Sonar?"

"Dr. Kendal's using it for a pregnant patient

that was brought in a short while ago," she explained. "We've been taking in patients for a few days and those brought in a few hours ago are ahead on the list."

"X-rays?"

"We've got a queue there too, Adam, and the tech has been working overtime. Everyone is urgent so we can't push him in."

Adam removed the scope from his ears and pressed the thumb and forefinger of one hand to his eyes. "All right. Put him on the list for a sonar. I want a full chest, concentrating on the area around the heart." He handed the chart to Leah before turning to the volunteer firefighter. "Frank, the sonar is just a precautionary measure, so don't start reading too much into it." He grabbed a tongue depressor and a penlight and gestured for Frank to open his mouth. Once he was done checking the airways, he replaced the mask. "Any headaches, numbness or tingling in your extremities?"

Frank nodded jerkily. "Feels like pricks under my skin and my head's killing me."

Adam gently probed the back of Frank's neck up into the base of his skull to check for injuries he might be unaware of. "Nausea, double vision?"

"Some," Frank rasped. "Eyes a bit blurry and I've had a couple dizzy spells."

Adam reached for the pressure cuff on the wall behind the bed. "Leah will set up a drip with antibiotics and put you on a nebulizer while we wait for sonar. I don't think we have anything to worry about, Frank. Your heart sounds fine but your lungs don't. In the meantime, I'm going to treat you for smoke inhalation, so I need you to relax and concentrate on that breathing."

"Need…to get…out there, Doc," the man rasped, looking alarmed. He struggled upright, his breathing even more labored as he panicked. "Can't stay. The fire… It's bad. Lorena…the kids… Mrs. Kershaw?"

"The deputies can handle that," Adam said firmly and quietly, expertly fitting the cuff around Frank's arm. "I promise. What I can also promise is that you're in no condition to go haring off to check on them. Let the deputies do their job." He looked at a couple firefighters hovering outside the cubicle as he inflated the cuff. "And the rest of the team can handle things without you for a while. Right, guys?"

There was a chorus of consent. "They're bringing in more guys from Portland and Seattle," one grimy man said. "We'll be okay, Frank. Just listen to the doc."

At their words, Frank blinked rapidly, briefly looking away as though overcome with emotion. He waited until Adam finished taking his blood pressure before rasping, "My…chest…hurts real bad, Doc."

"Your BP is elevated but that's a normal response to smoke inhalation," Adam assured him. "The chest pain is most likely related but we'll check to be sure. Try to give your vocal cords a break. They've been scorched." He turned to go and indicated with a slight head incline for Leah to follow. Once outside, he dropped his voice. "Give him two milligrams of midazolam and watch his breathing. If he gets too agitated, we might have to intubate him. Any luck on finding me some scrubs?"

"We sent one of the volunteers. Where should we bring it?"

Adam scrubbed his hands over his face and gave it a moment's thought. "Any shower available?" He badly needed a shower, sleep and food. Oh, yeah, and there were a few things he wanted to say to Ms. Jefferies that were burning on his tongue.

Leah immediately led him away from ER, down a passage toward the back of the hospital. "The Incident Command Center brought their own ablutions, so I'm sure no one will mind if you use the employee locker room."

"I know where that is," Adam said, reaching out to touch her arm. "You go back to Frank. He needs those meds." He was about to turn away when he thought of something. "Is it possible the volunteer can find me coffee? I'm going to need it black and strong. Really strong."

"I'll get right on it," she said, her gaze searching his face. "But Frank's right. You look tired. When last did you eat or sleep?"

He thrust a hand through his hair and gave her a grim smile. "It's been a while. Wilbur Pass is—God, there's nothing left," he muttered, referring to the area around his cousin's farm. "A lot of the folks up there have lost everything."

Her face paled. "Ben?" she asked quickly, her hand going to her mouth in distress. "Is Ben okay?"

"A couple of minor injuries," he told her, turning away. He didn't think he'd be able to talk about the devastation he'd lived through the past few days. "We managed to save the horses and most of the house but a lot of others weren't so lucky, Leah. Now would be a good time to pray for rain."

She swallowed and gave a short nod as Adam placed a hand on the door, but before he could push it open, she said quietly, "She's here."

Knowing instantly whom she was talking about, Adam tried to pretend ignorance as he gave her a confused look across his shoulder. "Who's here?"

Leah rolled her eyes and huffed out an annoyed breath. "Ms. Jefferies. But then you knew that, didn't you?"

"No, I didn't, but thank you for the heads-up." He shifted his weight and stepped into the doorway, Leah's quietly spoken words again stopping him in his tracks.

"What happened, Adam?"

After a couple of beats, he sighed and shoved impatient fingers through his hair. The previous burst of energy had drained away, leaving him exhausted. The last thing he wanted was to discuss Samantha—or his feelings—with anyone. "What do you mean?"

"She's hurting, although she tries hard to pretend nothing's wrong," she said, tilting her head to one side as she studied him with sympathetic eyes. "Sam looks as bad as you do and I can see she's heartsick and miserable. When she heard we hadn't seen or heard from you, she looked— terrified." Her eyes searched his. "I thought—"

"What?" he interrupted, suddenly furious at the shame that swamped him. Furious with Samantha for putting herself in harm's way and ashamed because her confusion and misery was his fault. "What *did* you think, Leah?" he demanded. "That a beautiful, sophisticated woman like Samantha would give up her pampered, privileged lifestyle for a half-breed, hick doctor from a small backwoods town like Juniper Falls? A man who doesn't have the time to give her what she deserves?" He exhaled in disgust, more at himself than at her. "Grow up," he snapped. "This isn't some inverted modern version of Cinderella."

For an instant, he saw hurt flash in her eyes only to be replaced by anger. "You know what?" she snapped, scowling at him. "I never thought I would say this, Adam, but you're a snob. You're the only one who sees yourself like that. And if you didn't have a chip on your shoulder, you'd notice that Samantha isn't the least bit pampered like all those spoiled, rich debutantes you like to date. She's warm and sweet and funny and the most unspoiled person I know, as well as the most generous." She paused to take a deep breath. "Not only did she donate a ton of medical supplies to the hospital and pushed the governor to establish Incident Control here in Juniper Falls, she organized water pumps and generators in case of a power failure and the tents out there for the firefighters and people who've been forced out of their homes. And no, she didn't tell me about everything she's done. I overheard the mayor and the sheriff talking. And aside from seeing that everyone out there has food, beverages and a place to rest, she's been helping out with the ward patients and comforting the children affected by the fires." She turned away from him and started down the passage, throwing, "Which one of your vain society princesses would do all that?" over her shoulder in a furious challenge.

Muttering a string of curses, Adam scrubbed his hands over his face. He didn't need to explain himself to anyone. He and Samantha were a disaster waiting to happen. Just look at his parents. They should never have met.

"Look, Leah," he said wearily to her departing back. "I don't expect you to understand but—"

She spun around. "I understand perfectly, Adam. The fact that you don't deserve her has nothing to do with who you are or where you're from. It's because you're punishing her for coming from the same world as your mother. And just in case you haven't figured it out. Samantha is *nothing* like the woman who handed you over to a man more interested in his broken dreams and the contents of a bottle than the innocent infant in his care." She didn't wait for a reply, her stiff back and stinging words leaving him with the sick feeling that she was right.

"Don't tell her I'm here," he called out gruffly.

Leah didn't reply but he thought he heard her mutter something uncomplimentary. Something that sounded like, "You're an ass."

CHAPTER THIRTEEN

MAYBE HE WAS an ass, Adam told himself as he stripped out of his soiled clothes and stepped into the shower, but that didn't discount the fact that he didn't want Sam anywhere near Juniper Falls. Not near him—where she would remind him of everything he would never have—and definitely not near the approaching fire.

By the time he left the locker room, dressed in clean scrubs, he was feeling a little more clear-headed. At midnight, this section of the hospital was quiet, so he quickly headed to ER and stuck his head through the door. When he saw that things seemed to have calmed, he went in search of food and coffee. No sense expecting anyone to wait on him.

Since he'd seen Samantha exit the tent with coffee for the deputy, he headed in that direction himself only to come up short when he saw her, laughing and chatting away with a group of dirty, sweaty firefighters like she was hosting a high society banquet.

The sight of her never failed to affect him in the most physical way. His heart began pounding, his gut clenched and he was sweating. When he realized he'd lifted a hand to rub at the ache beside his heart, he lost his legendary cool.

"What the hell are you doing here, Samantha?" he demanded when he was within earshot, the suppressed anger in his tone surprising not just her and the men surrounding her but himself, as well.

She gasped and spun around so fast, the man closest to her made a grab for her before she lost her footing. The sight of another man's hand on her, as well as the relieved joy filling her expression an instant before she masked her emotions, was like a blow to his chest. She hadn't however masked them quickly enough to hide the stunned hurt his words and tone caused.

The sight of that hurt, knowing he'd caused it—again—just made him angrier. And because he was angry at them both, he turned to the man wearing the vest identifying him as Incident Commander.

"Commander, I want her on the next helo out of here." He kept his voice low but she heard him, and her shocked gasp snapped his eyes back to her pale face and huge dark eyes.

She took a step backward and almost immediately, a couple of firefighters and a uniformed ranger surrounded her as though to protect her from his hostility. She ignored them, wide eyes on his as though she couldn't look away from the disaster unfolding around her.

He couldn't look away either. The instant they'd locked eyes, every emotion he'd struggled to deny came storming through him until he couldn't breathe.

From him, dammit. They were trying to protect her from him, and he hated that he'd been reduced to a jealous, insecure lover.

"Stop it," she hissed, finally pushing past the protective barrier of guys. "You're causing a scene. Go away and let me do my job."

No way in hell was he going away. Not now and maybe not ever. "And what job is that?" he demanded, unable to stop himself from wrapping his fingers around her arm and pulling her toward him. On some level, he recognized the over-large shirt as his, but the instant he drew her unique fragrance into his lungs, his mind went blank.

Through the roaring in his head, he heard a voice demand, "Who are you again?"

Someone stepped forward and clapped him on the shoulder, breaking the tension. "This is Dr. Adam Knight," Grey Larson, the new forest services area chief said, subtly nudging Adam away from Samantha. He'd gone to school with Adam, left for the military and returned to join the forest services. "He's a surgeon from San José but he grew up in the area and provides regular specialist medical care for the county. He's been helping out at Wilbur Pass."

Ignoring Grey and the commander, Adam turned to Samantha and growled, "Dammit, Samantha, this is no place for you."

"Why?" she demanded. "Because I'm some vain, useless debutante?"

Recalling Leah's accusation, he shook his head. "I never said that, Samantha. I don't think that."

"Don't you?" Her voice hitched alarmingly, making his heart clench in his chest. *Damn*. He hadn't meant to make her cry. He just wanted her safe. Away from the inferno of that hungry beast heading in their direction. The thought of what those monstrous flames could do to her soft silky skin had bile rising into his throat, choking the life out of him.

When he didn't reply, she took a deep breath and firmed her soft wide mouth. "You know what, Adam? Prejudice goes both ways."

He blinked away the horrifying images he'd seen over the past few days. "What the hell's that supposed to mean?"

Looking mad, she snapped, "I'm busy," and shoved past him. "You figure it out."

Stunned by that uncharacteristic show of aggression, Adam turned to stare after her departing figure, her back ramrod straight, her jeans-clad hips twitching and the air surrounding her practically snapping with fury.

Finally becoming aware of the silence behind him, Adam turned back to see a mix of curiosity, censure and amusement in the expressions of the men around him.

"What?" he snarled, exasperated and a little embarrassed to be caught eyeing Samantha's bottom in those skintight jeans when what he wanted was to bundle her up and put her on the first flight to safety. Okay, so maybe that wasn't *all* he wanted to do but having her safe and out of danger was suddenly an overriding drive.

"You are one dumb ass," Grey said sadly, shaking his head.

"Yeah," Adam sighed, scrubbing a hand down his face, wishing he could rub away the heavy feeling in his gut. "That's nothing new."

"So, Knight," the commander said, his eyes intent on Adam. "How're you at field trauma?"

Struggling against the urge to follow Samantha and demand to know what she'd meant, Adam tried to focus on the IC's words instead of the need to have her in his arms or kiss her until the anger and misery in her eyes turned soft and sleepy with desire. Until *his* anger and misery melted beneath the touch of her gentle hands and soft lips.

"I volunteered for the local search-and-rescue over the summer holidays while I was in med school. Why?"

"We have a situation," the commander, a middle-aged man with military bearing informed him. "One of the rangers was checking the fire lines near Coopers Canyon and fell about fifty feet into a gulley. We're fairly certain he's injured, just not how badly. We're short paramedics and no one trained in traumatic fall injuries." Even as he spoke, they could hear the sound of an approaching helo. "You okay to fly out, Doc?"

Adam wasn't okay but assisting on a rescue would be the perfect distraction. His emotions were out of control and he had no idea how to fix things with Samantha so she would leave. Glancing back over his shoulder, he caught the flash of long legs disappearing through the front entrance. He couldn't blame her because he'd been irrational when he was always the cool voice of reason.

There was nothing cool or reasonable about his feelings for Samantha and maybe it was time to settle things between them. He couldn't live like this anymore. Wanting her desperately and hurting them both because she was too good for him.

He sighed and accepted a cup of black coffee from Grey. There was always time after they'd brought in the ranger.

"Yeah," he said, taking a healthy slug of the strong, sweet brew, "I'm fine."

"Good," the commander said briskly. "I want you on that team."

The instant Samantha found herself in a quiet dimly lit hallway, she sank back against the wall and squeezed her eyes closed against the wild emotions swamping her—anger, hurt, love and joy all mixed up inside her, making her feel a little crazy.

And then because she needed to hide the furious tears slipping through her tight lids, she slapped a hand over her eyes and bit back a sob.

Dammit, dammit, *dammit!* Why on earth was she crying? What the heck was wrong with her that the mere sight of Adam—tall, darkly handsome and very much alive—had sent such joy and relief swamping her that her knees had almost buckled. Okay, so she'd nearly flung herself at him, but one glimpse of his furious expression had frozen her, the hurt slicing deep enough to wound.

Deep enough that she might never recover. God, she thought, rubbing her palms over her face to eradicate every evidence of tears. What the hell was she doing here? The past few days had been hell not knowing where he was or if he was okay. When she'd seen him stalking toward her, looking all rumpled and tired, his mouth pressed into a tight line of fatigue, she'd felt such a rush of relief that for a moment she'd been dizzy. But he'd been furious, yelling at her and demanding that she be put on the next flight out.

As if she were an errant child caught playing hooky.

Biting her lip, she fought the hurt and confusion pressing in on her. And even as she gently banged her head against the wall in frustration, anger began to build too because having people leave wasn't something new. Her parents, her siblings, her grandfather, Lawrence and now Adam. She didn't know what was wrong with her that caused them to leave, but that didn't mean she had to continually watch them do it.

Coming to an abrupt decision, Samantha spun around, mouth firm and shoulders straight. It would be okay, she told herself. She was strong and she was fine on her own. She certainly didn't need a man to make her feel complete.

Determined to ignore her crazy seesawing emotions, she headed to the tiny children's ward. There was always a little one needing a hug and a quiet story to banish their fears and heartache.

She just wished she could banish hers as easily.

* * *

Adam double-checked the injured ranger for shock and froze when the aircraft lurched sideways and then dropped before the pilot managed to wrestle the craft upright again. The wind was getting worse and he sent a wary look out the window and wondered if the red glow in the sky was a little brighter than before.

Powerful gusts of wind buffeted the aircraft, the air supercharged with dry crackling heat that seared his eyeballs and sent his hair lifting off the back of his neck. Whether from the static in the air or a foreboding, he didn't know. But he suddenly wished he'd insisted that Samantha leave Juniper Falls, maybe even bargained with the commander—his help in exchange for flying Samantha out. But even as he thought it, he knew he could never withhold his help even to save someone he loved.

Adam abruptly stilled. There was a sudden roaring in his head as though the universe were demanding his attention. Demanding he finally acknowledge what had been there all along.

Love. He loved Samantha with everything in him. And the thought of her in the path of those greedy flames terrified him. She was his. His heart—his only. And getting back to her was suddenly more important than his pride. More important than his life because he knew that without Samantha he had nothing.

He straightened, his eyes whipping to Grey's in the awful knowledge the instant before he felt it—felt the helo shudder. There was a terrible grinding noise as the craft was thrown sideways, tilting at an impossible angle as they plummeted into the darkness below.

Through the blood thundering in his head, he heard the pilot yelling, "Brace yourselves," and all Adam could think was that he'd been offered love—offered *everything*—and he'd walked away from it.

Sam carefully placed the sleeping toddler in the empty crib and after pulling the blanket over the little body, paused to brush the tangle of curls from the child's forehead. For just an instant, she mourned the fact that she would never have a child of her own, because the thought of having a baby with anyone but Adam seemed—abhorrent.

Maybe she should just get cats, she thought with a sad smile. Become the youngest cat lady in San José—

Abruptly, everything in her went on alert. Her head jerked up and she spun around to see Leah standing in the doorway. The med student's face was a mask of shock, her eyes huge and devastated in her pale face. Sam instinctively knew something terrible had happened to Adam.

An awful pressure built in her chest—her ears rang—and before she realized she'd moved, she was grasping Leah's arm and dragging her out of the children's ward. She stared at the younger woman, her throat tight with dread. She could barely voice the terrifying thoughts in her head.

"What happened?" she demanded, her heart seizing in her chest, her world narrowing down to this moment.

"It's Adam," Leah whispered, her throat working furiously. Her huge eyes swam with tears. "He went out with the rescue helicopter. It—" She broke off with a sob before continuing, her voice tight with fear. "It went down a half hour ago and—Sam, they have n-no idea if there are any s-survivors."

Sam's mind went blank. She heard the roar of white noise in her head, and the next minute, she realized she'd slid down the wall and Leah was shoving her head between her knees.

"Breathe, Sam," the younger woman ordered, her voice hitching with emotion. "B-breathe. Come on, in and out. Slowly. Don't give up on him. Just—*don't*." She said the words again and again, so softly it became a chant that filled Sam's head, surrounding her until she wondered if Leah said the words for Sam, herself or—or for Adam.

Oh, God. Adam.

An image of his broken body flashed into her mind, sending pain stabbing through her head. Her heart felt as though a giant fist were crushing that fragile organ and all she could think about was that she'd been a coward. She'd been so wrapped up in her own insecurities that she hadn't thought about how Adam felt. About *his* insecurities. He'd been rejected by his socialite mother and believed he wasn't good enough for Sam. But what he'd done with his life made her ashamed of herself, her fear of facing her feelings.

He'd blown hot and cold because she was always the one to pull back every time he got too close. She was afraid of the intensity of her feelings, afraid of risking her heart. Besides, what would such a strong, selfless man like Adam want with a woman who was too afraid to live, too afraid to love?

Because she *did*, she realized with blinding clarity. She loved him. With every breath in her body. With every beat of her bruised heart and she hadn't told him. Hadn't given him an inkling to how she felt because she was afraid of him walking away.

Now she might never get to tell him and the thought left her hollow. Empty.

And praying for a miracle.

Adam tucked his arm against his ribs and winced as he climbed one-handed down from the truck. He'd told their rescuers he was fine and had insisted on helping those in worse shape than himself, but he knew he had a cracked rib or two, a head wound that bled like a stuck pig and a laceration on his left bicep.

He would probably have a headache for a few days and he'd need a couple butterfly bandages.

The others hadn't been so lucky and Adam had done what he could, insisting the pilot, injured ranger and Grey be flown to Fresno. The pilot had sustained a serious head injury and Adam suspected Grey had a ruptured spleen and needed emergency surgery. The rest of the flight crew were like Adam—walking wounded—and could get medical care in Juniper Falls.

All he could think about, as he moved gingerly toward ER, was finding Sam and convincing her that she was his.

And then there she was, illuminated in the doorway. Adam froze, too afraid of what he might—or might not—see in the huge eyes locked onto his.

In the instant before he knew either of them

had moved, Adam saw more than he'd hoped for. Her eyes burned fever-bright, they almost glowed in the dim light. He saw terror at the blood and joy that he was alive. He saw relief and a love so huge he felt his throat close. Then Sam was flinging herself at him and he had to let go of his ribs to catch her.

Her body crashed against his and even as he winced against the pain radiating through his body, he was wrapping her in his arms as though he would never let her go. She buried her face in his sweaty, bloodied neck, and when he went to ease her away from him because she was everything that was sweet and fragrant, she gave an inarticulate protest and clung harder to him. For several long moments, he enjoyed the feel of her body against his.

He dipped his head to press a kiss to the top of her head and he felt her body shudder. And even before he heard the first sob, he felt the hot splash of her tears against his skin.

"Hey," he murmured, dipping his head to hers and burying his face in the wild tangle of soft hair. "I'm here," he murmured over and over, uncertain if he was reassuring her or himself that she was where he needed her.

Finally, the storm of weeping lessened and she loosened her hold. "I'm s-sorry," she hiccupped.

"I d-didn't m-mean to c-cry, Adam, but you s-scared me."

"It's okay, baby," he crooned softly, rubbing his cheek in her tousled hair, grateful to be alive if only for this moment. "I scared me too. Especially when I thought I might never get to hold you again." He shifted and pressed a kiss to her forehead but she ducked her head.

"Don't l-look at me," she said quickly. "I scare everyone when I cry."

He chuckled softly and nudged her chin until he was looking into eyes as damp as the early morning sky after a storm. "I don't scare easily, Samantha Jefferies. My ancestors were warriors."

"Oh, God," she sniffed, catching his wrist when he caught her tears with his thumb. "I must look awful."

Staring down into her familiar face, Adam felt his heart turn over in his chest. "You could never, Sam," he murmured, dipping his head to touch his lips gently to hers, tasting tears as well as home. "You're beautiful. Even when you cry."

Sam gave a watery laugh and let her lips cling to his. "You're a terrible liar, Adam Knight."

"Oh, baby," he rasped, love and relief crashing through him. "I wouldn't mind drying your tears for the next fifty years. You're beautiful. You'll always be beautiful to me."

Everything in her stilled. After a couple of beats, she lifted her head and pushed away a few inches so she could see his face.

Her eyes searched his. "What—what are you saying, Adam?"

"I'm such an idiot," he said roughly. "For trying to send you away when you belong right here. With me. I love you, Samantha Jefferies, and I'm not about to let you go."

Sam gasped, her eyes wide and a little shocked as she stared into his. The universe seemed to still. As though the very air was holding its breath. It was then that Adam realized they had a growing audience and they too seemed to be holding their breaths.

"You—you *love* me?" she gasped, looking stunned. As though she couldn't conceive that he might.

"Oh, yeah." He bent his head to crush her lips with his for a moment before sliding his mouth to her ear. "You don't think I make an idiot of myself or declarations like this every day, do you? Especially in front of an audience."

Sam gasped and whipped her head around to see the entire ER as well as all the firefighters and rescue crews all gathered around, watching the drama unfold.

"*Omigod*," she yelped, jumping back, her hand flying up to cover her flaming cheek. "Why didn't you tell me everyone was looking?" she squeaked. Her retreat brought her bumping into Adam, her elbow catching him right where a huge bruise was forming on his side. Pain exploded through him and lights exploded inside his head. He heard a muttered oath and felt himself falling.

Sam cried out and tried to catch him but he was a big man, taking them both down. From a distance, he heard someone barking out instructions in a voice tight with worry, then he was being lifted and carried.

When he next surfaced, bright lights burned against his eyelids and for just an instant, he was confused. Then his memory returned in a rush and he groaned. He'd passed out like a little girl—right at Sam's feet.

Way to go with impressing his woman.

"Adam," an imperative feminine voice demanded, "Can you hear me? Open your eyes before I call Aunt Coco." He groaned again and turned, taking in Samantha's pale worried face through eyes narrowed against the bright light. Her eyes were filled with fear—for him.

Her fingers jerked against his and he realized she was gripping his hand fiercely. Her breath hitched as it did when she was having a panic attack, "Breathe, baby," he croaked. "Look at me and take a deep breath."

"Dammit, Adam," she rasped, her throat working convulsively. "I'm not having a panic attack, and why didn't you tell me you were injured?"

For long moments, he stared at her, wondering if he'd entered an alternate universe. "Why?" he croaked, licking his parched lips.

There was a quick wrinkling of her brow as she lifted an ice cube to his lips. "Why what?"

His forehead tightened as he stared up into her face, noticing for the first time that she didn't have that wild panicked look in her eyes and her skin wasn't sheened with the perspiration that usually accompanied an attack.

His hand gripped hers and although her fingers trembled in his, her skin was warm silk. He frowned. "Why aren't you having an attack?"

She stared at him for a couple of beats as though he were insane. "You're lying here bleeding from a head wound and possible internal injuries and all you can worry about is whether I'm having a panic attack?"

He nodded, then winced when pain lanced through his brain. "It's just a couple of cracked ribs," he explained. "Nothing serious."

She gave a watery snort and brushed the hair off his forehead. "You're crazy, you know that?" And when he continued to watch her, her face flushed the wild rose that never failed to entrance him. "All right," she burst out, looking embarrassed. "I—I did have one but only at the thought that I might never see you again." She sucked in a deep breath and looked like she was about to admit to something heinous. "I love you, Adam," she admitted in a rush, her flush deepening and her eyes looking just a little bit panicked. "A warrior needs a woman who won't fall apart at the first sign of trouble." Her breath rushed out. "So, no more panic attacks for me."

His smile started small, just tugging the corners of his mouth. "God, woman. You have no idea how much I love you," he declared, joy filling him until he laughed and pulled her down to his mouth. "I don't care about your panic attacks, only that I'm there to help you through them. You're everything I dreamed of having for myself, Samantha. You make me feel like I'm finally home. Be mine." And then he was kissing her, coaxing her lips, reveling in the softness of her mouth, adoring the way her lips clung to his and desperate for the taste of her heart spilling into his mouth.

When he finally came up for air, he kept her close, secretly pleased with her ragged breathing. "Come home with me Sam." He kissed the corner of her mouth. "Build a life with me." He brushed his lips across her eyelashes. "Make a life with me—for at least the next fifty years."

She sucked in a sharp breath and pulled away,

eyes damp and luminous in her flushed face. "Oh, Adam."

"Forgive me for being a prejudiced idiot," he said fiercely, afraid that she would say she loved him but couldn't be with him. "I'm so in love with you I went a little crazy there for a while because all I could think about was that you were too good for someone like me. I panicked."

"Someone like you?" she asked gently, her face radiating love and joy as she cupped his face in her hand. "You mean a man who stole my heart despite my determination to remain heart-whole? A man who gives everything of himself to others because that's who he is? A man with more love, compassion and courage in his little finger than anyone I know?"

"Marry me, Sam," he coaxed softly, wondering for just an instant if he were dreaming. But her hand was warm and gentle on his face, her breath a brush of love. "I know I'm not much to look at and I don't have the pedigree of your Boston blue blood but I—"

Sam gently placed a finger against his lips, dipping down to replace it with her mouth. "You're everything, Adam," she murmured, her eyes shining with the force of her emotions. "And you're perfect for me."

A sound drew their attention, and they looked up to see the entire ER—and the rescue crews—

had followed them into the ER to blatantly eavesdrop. A couple of nurses sniffed, looking teary-eyed and several men wore huge grins.

"Thank God for our audience," Adam chuckled, palming the hand still cupping his cheek. His eyes caught hers. "With all these witnesses, you have to say yes."

Sam gave a watery chuckle and hid her face in his neck. "Yes," she murmured against his throat. "With you, it'll always be yes."

Adam couldn't prevent the grin that split his face.

"She said yes," he told the impatient crowd, and with the roar of approval embracing them both, he took her mouth in a kiss that began their future.

A future destiny had gifted him.

* * * * *

If you enjoyed this story, check out these other great reads from Lucy Ryder

Pregnant by the Playboy Surgeon
Resisting Her Commander Hero
Rebel Doc on Her Doorstep
Caught in a Storm of Passion

All available now!